THE AMAZING

VALVANO

and the Mystery of the
HOODED RAT

THE AMAZING

VALVANO

and the Mystery of the
HOODED RAT

Mary Robinson

Houghton Mifflin Company
Boston   1988

Library of Congress Cataloging-in-Publication Data

Robinson, Mary, 1939-
  The amazing Valvano and the mystery of the hooded
rat.

  Summary: Maria is excited about her plans to perform
a magic act in the school talent show until her pet
rat, an integral part of the act, is kidnapped.
  [1. Magicians — Fiction. 2. Mystery and detective
stories. 3. Talent shows — Fiction] I. Title.
PZ7.R56752Am 1988   [Fic]   87-26179
ISBN 0-395-44314-8

Printed in the United States of America

S 10 9 8 7 6 5 4 3 2 1

For Tom and John

Contents

THE AMAZING

VALVANO

and the Mystery of the
HOODED RAT

· 1 ·

The Death-Defying Act

I put on my cape, walked quickly through the doorway, then swept my arms out and shouted, "I'm the Amazing Valvano." The Amazing Valvano — that's my stage name. My real name's Maria Cecilia Valvano.

I was working on the entrance of my magic act. I wanted something dynamic — something hot — something that would knock the kids in my fifth grade class out of their seats.

I considered roller skates, but they wouldn't work. I'd have to take them off for the rest of the act. Too bad, because they'd make me look taller. My dad said I'd shoot up any day now, but a lot of days have gone by and I'm still the shortest girl in my class.

I put a chair in the middle of my bedroom and stood on it. I liked being up in the air. I felt powerful.

I shouted, "And now, the — help — oops!" I almost fell. It was too hard to shout and get off the chair at the same time. I kicked the chair and faced reality: I had to be introduced. Then I could stand in a small pool of light with my back to the audience, my arms held out from my shoulders so that everyone could see my beautiful red cape. At the right moment, I'd whip around, flaring the cape in the air.

I tucked my white satin shirt into my new black jeans and took my position. I introduced myself and spun around, taking an extra turn. I swept off my hat, took a deep bow, and pulled a bouquet of flowers out of the air. I liked it.

I wished my best friend Maxine McCollem would hurry up. This was our afternoon to hang out together. But first she had to stop at her parents' beauty parlor.

I changed into my old jeans and blue sweat shirt and brushed my short brown hair. I liked the way Maxine's mom had cut it: it made my dark brown eyes look big. Mom said for the show she'd teach me how to use make-up so my eyes would look even bigger.

Mom worked at Jim's Drugs and had learned a lot about using make-up. Whenever she got free samples she gave me and Maxine some to try out.

I went downstairs to Bud's corner store and told Bud I was going over to Maxine's for the rest of the afternoon. When Mom was working she made me tell him where to find me.

When I came out of the store Maxine was walking

down the street. No wonder she was late — she was using her magnifying glass on practically everything and was writing in the red notebook I had given her for her birthday.

She spotted me and ran the rest of the way, stretching her long legs so much her school uniform bunched above her knees. Maxine was tall and thin with dark curly hair and thousands of freckles.

"Look at this." She showed me her notebook. "It's Sister Margaret's handwriting. I'm collecting handwriting samples. How about one of yours?"

"As long as you don't convict me of anything."

One of the reasons Maxine and I were best friends was that we both knew what we wanted to be when we grew up: I was going to be a magician and she was going to be a detective. We'd promised to be best friends forever — like blood sisters. So far we'd been best friends for five years.

We walked across East Culver Street and down Russell Road to Maxine's house. I was glad we were alone. I wanted to talk to her about my magic act again.

"The announcement for the school talent show was posted today," I said. "This is your last chance to be in my act."

"I don't know. Are you still planning to use Lester?"

"Yes." Lester was my ex–pet rat and not one of Maxine's favorite animals.

"Does Joey know?"

"Not yet." Joey Perrella was Lester's new owner and sort of my boyfriend. And he was definitely not one of Maxine's favorite people.

"Does Joey have to be in the act?"

"I want both my best friends in the act."

The problem was that my best friends were tired of each other. That's why I'd started to see them separately. It wasn't the best solution because when I went alone to Joey's, Maxine got angry, and when I went to Maxine's, I couldn't play with Lester.

"I don't know." Maxine brushed dark curls off her face. "I'm busy with my detective work. Maybe I'll be in the tech crew like last year."

"You'll change your mind when you see what I've got. My act's hot — really hot. You have to give me a chance. I can show you tomorrow after school when Joey drops off Lester for the weekend."

"I don't —"

"Maxine, you have to."

"Well, all right. But I'm only coming to look."

Maxine unlocked the door to her apartment building. She lived on the second floor like me. Her room was off the living room and used to be for storage. That's why there were two huge armchairs in it.

Maxine had two bookcases for her collection of magnifying glasses and Sherlock Holmes books. She even had

a coat and hat like Sherlock Holmes. She liked to put
them on when she was thinking. She would sit in one
chair and pretend she was Holmes and I would sit in the
other and pretend I was Watson.

I hopped into my chair and said, "My mom's decided to
surprise my dad and get her driver's license." My dad
was in the merchant marine and away on a trip. "He's
not due back for three weeks."

"Wait till she's driving." Maxine put on her Sherlock
Holmes hat. "You'll be able to go on vacations and picnics.
That's great."

"Wrong. It's not great. Mom wants to visit her relatives
in Texas this summer. She thinks Texas is *so* wonderful.
She'd move there if she could convince Dad. She thinks
I'd stop getting detentions there. You ever been to Texas?"

"We never go anywhere." Maxine wrapped herself in
her Sherlock Holmes coat and fell backwards into her
chair.

"If you do my act with me and we win, you'll get to
go somewhere. The grand prize is a trip to Disneyland."

"All right, all right." Maxine started writing in her
notebook. "I said I'd come to look."

I snuggled down in my chair and thought about winning the grand prize.

The front door slammed and someone called out, "Hey,
you lucky dudes. I'm home."

"Oh, no," said Maxine. "It's Kevin."

Kevin was one of Maxine's older brothers — the worst one.

"I'm busy," Maxine called out, shutting her door.

Kevin yelled through the keyhole, "Verrrry interesting, my dear —"

"Go away." Maxine stuffed a sock in the hole.

Kevin turned the television on in the living room and yelled at the people in the soap operas.

When he turned the television off, we opened the door and peeked out. He had the phone in one hand, a sour cherry soda in the other, and a piece of beef jerky in his mouth. His short dark hair looked like the jerky he was chewing on: stiff, messy, and wet.

He mumbled into the phone, "Yeah. Got it. 1408 Telegraph Avenue. I'll be there." He went to the desk and took some money out of a drawer.

"Hey," yelled Maxine, running into the living room. "Mom left that for me."

Kevin sneered. "So — you can spare it. I bet Rat Breath's got tons of money." Ever since I trained Lester for my science project Kevin called me Rat Breath. "Tell Mom not to wait dinner for me — I'll be late," Kevin yelled from the front door.

"Don't stick me with that," said Maxine. "You know Mom wants you to leave your own note."

But Kevin was already out the door.

"Boy, is he disgusting," said Maxine.

We pushed our chairs to the window so we could see what was happening on the street. Kevin ran up East Culver toward Washington. We knew where he was going: to the video arcade.

"Hey, there's Joey," I said. "Who's that with him?"

Maxine stood up to see better. "It's Lily."

"That's strange. I thought I told Joey to take Lester to the vet."

"Looks like he took Lily instead."

"Don't be funny." I stood up to get a better look, too. "Mom told me to be sure Lester was checked out before he came to spend the weekend with us. She doesn't want him bringing bubonic plague or anything."

"And you wonder why I don't want to be in your act?"

"Look, Maxine. Lester's safe. He's also smart. Wait till you see what he's going to do in my act. It's very tricky — in fact it's even death-defying."

"Now that's something I have to see."

"You will — tomorrow afternoon."

A Once-in-a-Lifetime Offer

Joey's line was busy that night so I had to wait until the next day to talk to him. I missed him in the morning and still hadn't talked to him by P.E., but I was determined to catch him before school got out.

The trouble was my locker door wouldn't open. I kicked it to get it unstuck. After four years of being on the soccer team, I had a good kick. I also had less than five minutes to change out of P.E. shorts and get to my next class.

I kicked again. The door sprang open and a pile of crumpled papers, books, and dirty clothes fell on my foot.

"Nice trick, Maria," said Maxine, joining me. "Are you doing that in the talent show?"

"Don't be funny. I'm still expecting to see you this afternoon." I pulled on the white blouse and blue plaid skirt of my school uniform.

"I'll be there, but I'm not thrilled."

"C'mon. You're going to like my idea — we'll be the hit of the show." I shoved the rest of my stuff back into the locker and quickly fluffed my hair.

As we hurried to Friday afternoon's last class, Joey caught up to us. "I can't wait to be in the talent show," he said. "I wish I could do more than one act." Joey bounced and moved his arms while he talked. "I could have Lester do tricks. What do you think of the curtain opening and me standing in a spotlight with a piece of cheese on my shoulder — then, on a drum roll, Lester runs out of the wings, up my arm, and eats the cheese?"

"Oh, wow," said Maxine, faking a yawn.

"It's great," I said. "But I've been trying to get ahold of you to tell you my hot idea for an act. You *have* to be in it and so does Lester. Can you drop Lester off at three and come back at four?"

"Hey, wait," said Joey. "You weren't listening. I want to do an act with Lester."

"But my act's better, I know it is. It's so good we can win an Academy Award, an Olympic medal, even a Nobel Prize. The only thing is you *have* to follow my plan."

"Sure, your plan." Joey shrugged. "You always have a plan."

"And we're always in it," added Maxine.

"I'd like a little gratitude once in a while," I said.

Lately, they hadn't been too excited about my ideas. "Besides, this is a once-in-a-lifetime offer. You can't turn it down."

"Yes, I can," said Joey.

"Me, too," added Maxine.

"But you won't. Be at my house at four o'clock sharp. You can stay till six. My mom's going to be late. She has a driving lesson after work."

"Okay," said Joey. "Just remember — I've only agreed to look at your act."

"Hey! Where do you think you are — at a party?" called Sister Margaret from our classroom doorway. "Hurry up. You're late again."

As I passed her she raised her eyebrows and said, "You're always where the action is, Maria."

On the way inside, Joey swung his shoulders like Sister Margaret. A few kids laughed and she turned around but didn't catch him. She gave him a knowing look, though.

When we sat down, she said, "I trust you've all seen the announcement for our school's annual talent show. Now, I want three fantastic acts from this class, and I mean fantastic — no martial arts, lip-synching, or imitations of me." She rocked back on her heels and gave Joey another knowing look.

She opened her black leather notebook. "You can tell me today or Monday what you'd like to do. Acts from my fifth grade class have always gone on to represent Saint Anne's school in the finals and I expect you to continue the tradition. This year's prize is a trip to Disneyland. Which one of you is going to win it?"

Hands shot into the air. I waved mine so hard I almost fell on the floor.

"Yes, Maria Valvano, what can you do?"

"A magic act, Sister."

"When did you learn magic?" whispered Reggie Jones, who sat next to me.

"She thinks she's an expert on everything," whispered Mary Louise O'Brien, the biggest pain in the whole school.

"I'm the Amazing Valvano." Murmurs spread through the class. "I can do mental telepathy, make things disappear, pull scarves out of the air." I had gotten a book on magic for my birthday. Since then I'd worked on my act, waiting for the date of the talent show to be announced.

"Just don't reveal what's on Monday's history test," said Sister Margaret. "Next."

"Lily and I will tap-dance," said Mary Louise, without waiting to be called on.

Everyone groaned. Those two had already won prizes for math, spelling, and writing. It wouldn't be fair if they won the talent show, too.

Joey stamped his feet as if he were tap-dancing. He

flung his legs across the aisle and tossed his head. On the last stamp, he threw out his arms.

"I'm surrounded by talent," said Sister Margaret, clapping. "Do you want to dance, too?"

"No, Sister. I'd like to sing a few songs."

Everybody laughed. Joey made up songs for girls he liked. The trouble was they all sounded like "Oh, baby, baby."

"Good luck," said Sister Margaret. "You can always change your mind."

Even Maxine laughed. I wished I could perform *real* magic and make her and Joey friends. My act was the last chance. I pictured us onstage — me in front in my new black jeans and white silk blouse, pulling a rabbit out of my hat and twirling around with my red cape flying through the air.

In back of me would be Joey and Maxine, tall and strong, carrying out my commands instantly. My act *had* to win. It *had* to be selected. There were just a few problems. I didn't have a rabbit — all I had was a rat — and Maxine and Joey didn't want to be in my act. But I could solve those details. After all, I was the Amazing Valvano.

"Start practicing this weekend," said Sister Margaret. "Next Friday I'll screen acts to make sure they're suitable. The audition will be the following Wednesday — acts will be selected then."

I wanted to go home and get the act ready for Joey and Maxine, but Sister Margaret had more for us to do. "Get into your math groups and begin work on page sixty-four."

When I opened my binder, a picture of Lester fell out onto the floor.

"I could make a lot of money with a rat like this," said Reggie, grabbing the picture.

"You stay away from Lester," I whispered, trying to get the picture back.

"That'll be easy," said Reggie. "He looks just like you."

"Let me see," whispered Mary Louise, dropping her book as she pushed closer. Reggie kicked her book under my chair. I grabbed the picture back.

"Watch out," whispered Maxine, but it was too late. Sister Margaret was walking straight toward me. "Give me that picture, Maria Valvano, and wait for me in the hall."

· 3 ·

An Impossible Promise

Sister Margaret walked out into the hall, her large shoulders swinging back and forth. The top of her black habit fluttered like a flag.

"Maria, what's going on? This is the third time this week you've disrupted the class." She looked at Lester's picture and pursed her lips. "Didn't you sell this rat to Joey?"

"I did but I miss him, Sister. He's coming to my house for the weekend. I have to get Mom to like him and I *have* to do something to make Maxine and Joey friends. I—"

"Get your priorities straight, young lady," said Sister Margaret. "Work those problems out on your own time. When you're in school, *pay attention*." She lowered her voice. "I know you can do a lot better in your studies and I expect a change by the end of the year." She handed me the picture. "Leave this at home. Otherwise, I'll *have* to give you another detention."

"I will. I promise, Sister."

I met Maxine by the lockers when school got out.

"Are we still coming to your house or did you get a detention?" she asked.

"No detention — you have to come."

Maxine stuffed papers and clothes into her backpack. "When are you going to forget about Lester? He isn't even your rat anymore."

"After we win the talent show. I promise. Unless Mom lets me buy him back." I banged my locker shut for emphasis.

"Forget it, Maria. You'd need a miracle for that to happen."

We pushed our way through the crowd of kids to the back hall and out into the school yard. Reggie ran by us and yelled, "The Amazing Valvano — ha! Bet your act stinks."

"What a pain," said Maxine.

"I think he's kind of cute. Look at his big brown eyes. His dark curly hair. He even has shoulders."

"Oh, barf. He hangs out with Kevin. They're either at my house eating all the good stuff or at a video parlor."

Reggie ran up to Kevin by the gate. Kevin yelled, "Rat

Breath a magician! That'll be the day." They ran off laughing.

Kevin was only a year older but he was the tallest kid in school. And if you asked me, he was also the ugliest.

Maxine and I walked up West Culver to Washington Street where my mom worked at Jim's Drugs and Maxine's parents had their beauty shop.

"Want me to come home with you and help?" asked Maxine.

"No, I want you to be surprised."

"Have it your way. I'll be at the shop." She ran down the street to Evalina's Beauty Affair.

I walked down East Culver Street to my house, concentrating so hard on arguments to convince Maxine and Joey to be in my act that I didn't notice Ernie Shapiro unloading bread from his delivery truck.

"Jeez, watch out," yelled Ernie, stopping me just in time from walking into a large box on the sidewalk. "I thought these overalls were supposed to make people notice me." The overalls were bright orange and said BORDESSA'S BAKERY in green letters on his chest and back.

"They do, they do. But there's something more important: the talent show's going to be in three weeks. Maxine and Joey are coming over to see my act in less than an hour. What if they don't like it?"

"Then they're crazy. You're a natural. I know — you listen to me."

Ernie had been a magician when he was young and he'd been teaching me magic tricks.

"But Joey wants his own act."

"Hey, wait till he sees yours before you start to worry." He lifted a box of bread. "But if you need any help, just call me. I'll do whatever you want." He walked up the steps into Bud's corner store.

I wished Maxine and Joey would say that.

I tapped on the store window to let Bud know I was home.

When I turned around, Joey was crossing the street with Lester. He handed me the cage and said, "See you at four."

I let myself into the building and ran upstairs to our apartment.

"I missed you, Lester," I said, putting his cage on the desk in my bedroom.

He peeked out of the box I'd lined with rags and a piece of rug, then crawled onto the upper platform in his cage. His little pink nose twitched madly the whole time. Lester had white fur, pink ears, pink feet, and even a hairless pink tail with a kink in the middle. He was my kind of rat.

"Time to exercise." I gently pulled him out of the cage. For a moment he hung onto the bars with his feet, then blinked his dark eyes and ran across my bedroom floor.

I set my magician's table and trick box in the middle

of the room and put all the props I'd need on my desk. While I read through the script, Lester cuddled between my feet.

I'd made his costume from fake fur left over from Dad's Santa suit. It was easy to make because I'd used Velcro to hold it together and an old shoulder pad of Mom's to shape the back.

When everything was ready I put Lester back in his cage and changed into my magician's costume. I was bowing in front of the mirror when the bell rang.

Joey came in singing, "Oh, I just want to be great, oh, oh, oh." He held the last "oh" for a long time. "Like it?"

"At least it doesn't have 'baby' in it."

"It does! Want me to sing that part?"

I was saved by the bell.

Maxine's eyes widened as she walked around me. "You look like a star. If I'm in the show, I want to look great, too."

"There's more to being a magician than wearing a costume," said Joey.

I pulled a scarf from his nose.

"Hey!" he said. "You're good."

"I can do this, too." I separated and joined three magic metal rings.

"Let me try," said Joey. I showed him and Maxine how the rings worked.

While they practiced I got the script.

"We're going to be 'The Amazing Valvano and Friends,'" I said.

"I like it," said Maxine, nodding her head.

"How about you?" I looked at Joey.

"It's not bad. But there's no guarantee I'll be in your act. The talent show could be the start of my singing career."

Maxine rolled her eyes. "You have as much chance for a singing career as I have for —"

"Maxine, please," I begged and handed Joey the script.

"You can't do mental telepathy," said Joey. "You have to be born being able to do it."

"It's a trick like the rest of my act. Only it's easier because I know the answer before I'm asked the question."

"How?" asked Joey.

"With your help. You'll write down people's questions on your clipboard while they write their answers and put them in envelopes. You'll put the envelope with the answer to the first question on the bottom of the pile instead of the top.

"When you ask the first question, I'll guess and probably get it wrong. The audience will like that. Then I'll pretend I'm checking the answer but in reality I'll open the second envelope and read the answer to the second question. I'll get the second question right and when I open an envelope to check the answer, I'll read the answer to the third question."

"I see," said Joey. "Whenever you open an envelope, you'll be reading the answer to the next question. I like it."

"Me, too," said Maxine. "People *will* think you're amazing."

Joey took Lester out of his cage and ruffled his fur. Then Joey and Maxine continued to read the script.

"Here's where you come in, Lester," said Maxine, patting his head. "You get pulled out of a hat."

Lester looked at us, twitched his pink ears, then chewed on his back foot.

Joey jumped up. "It says here that you're going to saw Lester in half!"

"Right," I answered.

"Wrong." Joey slammed his hand on the table.

"He can stay here while I teach him —"

"No way," said Joey. "He's not going anywhere. He's going to stay home in his cage."

"You sound like my father," said Maxine.

Lester stared at us as if he knew we were talking about him. I held up his costume.

"Now, *that's* amazing," said Maxine.

"Maria, he's not your rat anymore." Joey stuffed his hands into his pockets and frowned. "I said he could visit you once a month. Now you want to saw him in half."

"Don't worry, the trick's foolproof. I promise. He's not

even going to be in the box when I'm sawing. The box has a secret panel for taking him out." I pressed the Velcro together. "See. People will think he's a bunny."

"He looks dumb," said Joey.

"Not really," said Maxine. "He's kind of cute."

"Dumb! Dumb! Dumb!" yelled Joey.

"Watch out or you'll hurt his feelings. I think he likes his costume."

Lester looked at me and twitched his nose again.

"See," I said.

"He can't move," said Joey.

Lester fell over.

"That way he won't escape. Don't be so negative."

Maxine went to the back of my bedroom. "If I squint my eyes, he looks like a rabbit slumped on the floor."

"Why Lester?" asked Joey, picking him up and petting him.

"I'm a magician. I have to pull a rabbit out of my hat. All the real rabbits I know are too big." I put Lester in my hat, twirled around with my cape flying, then executed a deep bow and pulled Lester out into the air.

"Was that great or was that great?" I asked.

"Great," said Maxine, trying on my cape. "You're a terrific magician."

"Yeah. She's great," agreed Joey. "But that doesn't mean I have to let Lester be in her act."

"We'll be stars," urged Maxine. "How can you turn

us down? You know your singing's nowhere near as good. Neither are Lester's tricks. We have a chance to win. Let's go for it."

"Maybe. Let me see the box."

"Be careful. It's Ernie's trick box. He made it himself." I demonstrated the secret panel in the back and the secret compartments in the bottom.

While Joey examined the snaps and locks, Maxine and I looked at each other. We knew we had him.

"Think of all the rides you could go on," she whispered.

"Think of what your parents will do when you're the hit of the show," I added.

"Okay. All right," he said. "You guys are too much. I'll do it—as long as nothing happens to Lester."

"Lester will be fine," I promised. But how was I to know my promise would be impossible to keep?

· 4 ·

A Big Emergency

Mom came home with her face flushed and her dark curly hair standing up in spikes off her forehead. She waved her driver's handbook at us. "There's all these rules I have to learn — like homework. My teacher says I have a natural instinct for the road. Most people need ten lessons, but I may need only eight."

"Great, Mrs. Valvano," said Joey, giving her a winning smile. "See you tomorrow, Maria."

Mom ruffled his hair, then hugged Maxine as she left. "Tell your mother I'll be taking her for a ride soon."

I followed Mom to the kitchen and waited until she'd made a cup of tea. "Guess what? Joey and Maxine want me to do a magic act with them and Lester for Saint Anne's talent show."

"Oh?" Mom's smile vanished.

"We could be the hit of the show. And Sister Margaret needs a hit, she said so."

"What are you getting at, Maria?" Mom pushed her hair up, making more spikes.

"Lester has to stay here until the show. It's only three weeks."

"Three weeks! Don't you remember why we got rid of him? He was always escaping. And his smell — I couldn't stand it then and it's probably worse now." She yanked her hair off her forehead. "I might have known these visiting rights would bring problems."

"If I do the act, Sister Margaret will think I've reformed."

Mom looked ill.

"Please. I'll keep my room clean and my uniform ironed. I'll test you every night on your driving questions."

Mom sighed. "You really think Sister Margaret's going to like your act?"

"Yes, oh, yes." I jumped up and down. "The grand prize is a trip to Disneyland. And —"

"Enough. You always have an answer for everything. Lester can stay — but if he causes any trouble at all, he goes right back to Joey's. I mean it."

"Thanks, Mom." I hugged her as hard as I could. "You won't even know he's here."

On Saturday Joey, Maxine, and I worked on the act. Things were going fine until Joey wanted to do a solo trick. Then Maxine did too.

"There's barely enough time for my tricks," I said. "Besides, it's my act, I get to do the solos."

"You get to do all the good stuff," said Maxine.

"Yeah, why not call your act 'The Amazing Valvano and Her Slaves'?"

"C'mon, you guys. I'm including you in my act."

"Big whoop," said Joey and he sat down on my bed.

"I need a break," said Maxine. "I'm going home for lunch."

"Good idea." Joey pulled on his jacket faster than he'd moved all morning. "See you in an hour."

I figured once they knew the act things would be better.

While they were gone I aired out my bedroom so Mom wouldn't complain about Lester's smell. I even made sure to put Lester back in his cage before he did anything on the rug or my bedspread.

When Maxine came back, we practiced the card trick.

"Take a card, any card," I said. "The Amazing Valvano will tell you what it is."

"This is the fifth card," said Maxine. "If you don't guess right, I think you should forget this trick. And you could think about letting me — your best friend — do a solo."

"Queen of spades. I just know it."

"Wrong."

"Six of clubs."

"Wrong again."

"Nine of —"

"Pull a scarf out of your nose," said Maxine. "You do that best of all."

"Okay, we forget the card trick." I threw the cards on my desk. "But I'm the only one who's doing solos."

On Sunday, at the end of the afternoon, Joey said, "Well, that's it for me today." He put Lester in his cage and headed for the door.

"Wait a minute," I said. "Lester has to stay here until the show."

"Oh, no, he doesn't," said Joey.

"You agreed to that."

Joey looked at Maxine. She shrugged.

"Yes, you did," I said. "When you agreed to be in the show. I said, 'He can stay here while I teach him —'"

"You did not," shouted Joey.

"I did too."

"Did not."

"I did too and anyhow he has to stay here because I'm head of the act."

"I don't believe it," said Joey. "Okay, he stays. But after the show, don't plan anything else for me or Lester." He banged the door as he left.

On Monday more kids signed up for acts. Reggie Jones surprised everyone when he said, "I'll juggle."

"What?" asked Sister Margaret.

Maxine sent me a note:

HE CAN'T JUGGLE. HE ONLY THROWS KIDS' THINGS IN THE AIR.

"Balls, bowling pins, knives —"

"Forget the knives," said Sister Margaret. "Just bring your balls and bowling pins."

Even though Reggie could be a pain, I liked his style.

During math, Mary Louise whispered, "My braces are going to be off in time for the show."

"So?"

"You don't have a chance to beat us."

"You wish. You wait —"

"Maria!" said Sister Margaret. "Remember what I said about paying attention."

"Yes, Sister."

I tried to pay attention, but Mary Louise smirked every time I looked at her. During English, she whispered, "You'd better not use Lester in your act or I'll tell Sister Margaret that you have an unfair advantage."

"Why don't you mind —"

"Maria! I'll see you in detention this afternoon," said Sister Margaret.

By the time I got home from detention it was too late to rehearse.

*   *   *

Tuesday afternoon we did the whole act without looking at the script and on Wednesday we had our own dress rehearsal. We were on the road to success. We went out for an ice cream to celebrate.

After dinner on Wednesday I was talking to Maxine on the phone when Mom yelled, "MARIA!"

I ran to the living room, where she'd been taking a nap.

"When I woke up, he was sitting on my chest, staring into my face. He — he . . ." she sputtered.

"I'm sorry, Mom. I was on the phone. I thought I closed my bedroom door."

"He was breathing right into my face. Goodness knows what kind of germs are in his breath." She kept brushing off her chest.

"He's clean. He washes every day." I couldn't see Lester. He must have run off when Mom screamed.

"I breathed in his germs. And his smell was revolting — like your room. Eaahh!" Mom shuddered, then yelled, "There he is. Get him!"

Lester ran out from behind the front window curtain and scurried toward the piano. I cut him off by the television set and caught him.

"That's it, Maria. He goes back to Joey's tomorrow afternoon."

The next day Joey acted so smug when I told him about

Lester that I called off the afternoon's rehearsal and arranged to be with Maxine. I was going to drop Lester off at Joey's on my way to her house.

When I got home from school, the door to my building was unlocked. Mom was going to be annoyed. She was captain of the neighborhood crime-watch group and she'd told our landlord to secure our building. He was supposed to make sure the front door closed automatically.

I continued upstairs to our apartment. When I got to the landing, the front door was open. I ran inside, yelling, "Hey, I'm home." But nobody answered.

The apartment was so quiet I raced through to see if anything had happened. The television and VCR were still in the living room. So was the stereo. Everything looked the way it usually did until I got to my bedroom. My throat tightened when I saw the mess. Drawers were open. My clothes were thrown on the floor. And worst of all, Lester's cage was gone.

A trail of shredded newspaper led to the hall. I was following the trail when I heard the front door close. I raced down the hall and out the door. Heavy footsteps clomped down the stairs ahead of me. When I got to the landing where the stairs turned, the downstairs door slammed shut.

"Help! Police!" I yelled, and jumped down the remaining steps. When I ran outside no one was on the street, not one person.

I staggered out of breath into Bud's corner store. Bud was talking to Mrs. Bossi, the neighborhood know-it-all. "Did you see someone leave my apartment?" I shouted.

"Lots of kids just walked by," said Bud. "On their way home from school."

"Not them. Did you see anyone else — less than a minute ago?"

Bud slowly zippered his gray sweat shirt and thought. Mrs. Bossi glared at me. Whenever she twitched her shoulders, the blue parrots on her dress fluttered.

"No," said Bud. "Can't say that I did."

"What's the matter?" asked Mrs. Bossi.

"Nothing."

"It certainly seems that something's the matter. You interrupted our conversation without so much as an 'excuse me' and now you look as if you've seen a ghost. What's going on?" The blue parrots were flying across her chest.

"I can't explain now." I knew she'd tell Mom I was rude, but if I told Mrs. Bossi what had happened, she'd tell everyone else in the neighborhood.

As I ran upstairs the phone rang. It was Mom, calling from her job at Jim's Drugs.

"Did you take Lester back to Joey's?"

"No, I can't — I —"

"No excuses, young lady. Change your uniform and do it."

"But, Mom, Lester's gone."

"Not again. Find him. And when you do, bring him right over to Joey's."

"But, Mom —"

"No more buts. I'm up to my ears in the inventory sale. I have a driving lesson after work, so put the lasagna in the oven at five-thirty. Don't forget, because I have to leave early for the slide show at the church tonight."

"Yes, Mom."

The phone rang again as soon as I hung up.

"What's taking you so long, Maria?" It was Maxine. "This is the only afternoon Kevin isn't going to be home."

"Come over right away," I said. "And bring your detective kit. We have a big emergency on our hands — Lester's been kidnapped!"

· 5 ·

The Mystery of the Hooded Rat

Maxine ran upstairs with a magnifying glass in one hand and a pair of plastic gloves in the other. "Put these on so you don't disturb any fingerprints." She pulled her red notebook out of her backpack, sat down on the top step, and commanded, "Tell me everything."

"The downstairs door wasn't closed," I began. "That's how the kidnapper got into the building. And the kidnapper knew about the hidden key to the front door. It's still in the lock."

Maxine sprinkled powder on the key, pressed a piece of tape on it, and put the tape in her notebook. "Too bad. Blurry prints." She aimed her instant camera at me. "Point to the lock. We need pictures of the scene of the crime. All detectives do this."

"Well, okay. Could you wait till I put on my new sweater?"

"No — just stand there."

We took turns taking pictures of each other on the landing, in the hall, and in my bedroom. The pictures came out great, especially the one of me holding the phone. You can see how short my new haircut is. My hair's the same color brown as Mom's but it's straight like Dad's. I have dark skin like Mom, too. People are always asking me where I got my tan.

I look impressive in that picture — as if I'm on an important telephone call.

"Hey! Should I call Joey?" I asked.

"No rush." Maxine tossed a box of plastic bags on my desk. "Evidence bags. Save anything important."

"He'll be furious. He said Lester could stay here as long as nothing happened to him. He —"

"Not your fault."

Maxine talked funny when she was in her detective mode. She put the pictures in a bag and wrote the date on a stick-on label. Since she was tall and thin she could search everywhere, the top shelves of my bookcases and even the windowsill behind my desk.

"I can't stand it," I said. "I'm going to call Joey."

"I'd rather have a video camera."

"*C'mon*, Maxine. We've got to question people and search for Lester. We need Joey's help for that. And if we don't start soon, Lester will be lost forever."

"Look, Maria, I've read all the detective handbooks and I know what we should do and the order to do it in. We have to look for clues, record information, make a list of suspects —"

I glanced at my desk. Something clicked.

"Maxine, wait a minute. My cape is missing. I left it on the chair this morning. And look, all the magic act props have been moved: my boots, the scarves, even the box with the saw."

I got our script and went through the prop list. Besides Lester and my red cape, the kidnapper had taken the metal rings, my magician's hat, and Lester's rabbit costume.

"Maybe the kidnapper's going to do an act with Lester," said Maxine. "But who? And why?"

"That's what we have to find out," I said and dialed Joey's number.

"Dang," said Joey when he saw my bedroom. "This place has been seriously searched. Was there a ransom note?"

"Not yet." I was relieved he didn't blame me for the kidnapping. "I hope they don't want much. I've only got twelve dollars."

"I have twenty." He put his tool kit and a book about rats on my desk. "But I'll spend anything to get Lester back."

Joey looked as though he might cry. I felt that way, too. Poor Lester. He didn't deserve to be kidnapped.

"I need someone to diagram this room," said Maxine.

Joey got his tape measure. While he measured, I marked on the graph paper, and Maxine asked questions: "Who knew where your mom hid the front door key?"

"Almost everyone in the neighborhood, but not everyone knew Lester was here. He came last Friday and today's Thursday. He was here less than a week."

Maxine wrote *SUSPECTS* on a piece of poster board. "We need identifying information, plus a motive for the kidnapping."

Joey and I yelled: "Mary Louise." "Mrs. Bossi." "Reggie."

Maxine said, "Suspect number one is my disgusting brother." She wrote:

> KEVIN McCOLLEM — 12
> 6th grade
> tallest boy at Saint Anne's
> thin
> dark brown hair
> evil gray eyes
> ugly
> MOTIVE — MONEY

That summed up Kevin all right.

"He's in debt right now," continued Maxine. "He always said kids would pay money to see Lester do tricks."

"He used to be my friend," said Joey.

"But he stopped being your friend when I sold Lester to you and not to him. He said some day we'd be sorry."

"He knew Lester was here," said Maxine. "*And* he got out of school at noon today. You couldn't ask for a better suspect."

Joey pulled a picture of Kevin out of his wallet and taped it to the board. "If he's the kidnapper, I'll —"

"Wait a minute," I interrupted. "Mary Louise would do anything to win the talent show."

"I heard her complaining to Sister Margaret that we had an animal in our act," said Joey. "But Sister said it was okay for us to do that."

"See what I mean? Mary Louise had to kidnap Lester to stop us."

Maxine wrote:

MARY LOUISE O'BRIEN — 11
  5th grade
  short
  frizzy blond hair
  blue eyes
  braces
  gets all A's
  most repulsive girl at Saint Anne's
  MOTIVE — KNOCKING US OUT OF THE
  TALENT SHOW

I got our class picture and cut out Mary Louise's head to tape to the board.

"What about Mrs. Bossi?" asked Joey. "She never liked Lester."

"She was in the store talking with Bud," I said. "She couldn't have done it."

"What about Reggie?" asked Joey. "He said he knew a lab that would pay good money for a smart rat like Lester."

"Yeah, he told me he could make a lot of money from a rat like Lester. I thought he was just teasing me."

Maxine wrote:

> REGGIE JONES — 11
> 5th grade
> medium height
> short curly black hair
> dark brown eyes
> scar on chin
> MOTIVE — MONEY

"I told you he was disgusting," said Maxine, taping Reggie's cutout picture to the chart. "And Kevin would have told him Lester was here."

"Anyone else?" asked Joey.

"Lily Nakamura," said Maxine.

"No, she wouldn't steal Lester," said Joey, blushing.

Why was he blushing? Nobody liked Mary Louise and

Lily. They were too smart and pretty. They did everything together. They even walked the same way. The only difference was that Lily was shy and Mary Louise did all the talking.

"Mary Louise is her only friend," said Maxine. "Lily would do anything for her." She wrote:

> LILY NAKAMURA — 10
> 5th grade
> short
> short straight black hair
> black eyes
> braces
> glasses
> too smart
> MOTIVE — STAYING FRIENDS WITH
> MARY LOUISE

Joey blushed as Maxine taped Lily's picture on the chart. And I thought he liked *me*. Then I remembered Joey walking with Lily last week.

"Anyone else?" asked Maxine.

Joey shook his head.

I grabbed my jacket. "Let's interrogate these suspects now. I want to find Lester fast — before anything happens to him."

"Wait a minute." Maxine stopped us. "We have to re-enact the crime first."

Joey groaned.

"Why?" I asked.

"My guide says so. We must have a solidly based investigation. We can't afford to be sloppy."

Joey volunteered to be the kidnapper. Maxine and I took notes.

"Very interesting," she said. "The kidnapper had to have something to carry Lester's cage and the props in — like a large bag or a box. That's something a witness would remember."

"Lily and Mary Louise left school early today," I said. "And Lily was carrying a big bag. I—"

"Hey! Look at this." Joey picked up a piece of paper. "It's a drawing of Lester with something on his head and a mark down his back."

I took the paper. "It's not mine. I bet the kidnapper did it. What's this thing on Lester's head supposed to be?"

"Looks like a hood," said Maxine. She wrote *The Secret of the Rat's Hood* in her notebook.

Joey looked through his book. Ever since he bought Lester he'd been studying up on rats.

"Looks like a hangman's hood," I said. "You don't think Lester's going to be killed?"

"No," said Maxine. "The kidnapper would have killed Lester here and there's no blood."

"Blood!" My stomach jumped.

Maxine crossed out what she had written and wrote

The Case of the Missing Blood.

"Look," said Joey, showing us a picture of a rat with dark hair on its head and back. "This is a hooded rat!"

Maxine looked at the drawing with her magnifying glass, then crossed out what she had written again and wrote *The Mystery of the Hooded Rat.* "My first real case. I've been waiting for this moment all my life."

Joey and I exchanged looks.

"Look," I said. "We're a team — we have to work together."

"Lester needs us," said Joey.

"Right, we're a team," said Maxine, closing her notebook. "And we're ready to roll — it's time to go after suspects. I'll take Kevin."

"I'll take Mary Louise," I said.

"I'll take Reggie," said Joey. "And on the way to the arcade I'll question Lily."

This time when he said Lily's name he didn't blush, but he was trying to look cool and I knew it. I knew Maxine knew it, too.

"Her house isn't on the way to the arcade," I said.

"I know. I have to pick up some stuff at home first." He looked away.

As we walked downstairs Maxine read from her detective's guide. " 'Look into the eyes of the person you're questioning. If the eyes waver or turn away, that means the person is lying. Also, if the person is too eager to answer questions or is too helpful that can mean the person is lying. Also —' "

"We've got the message," I said, staring at Joey. "Let's meet back here in an hour. If one of us finds something important, call the others."

"One more thing," said Maxine. "If you think a suspect is holding back information, lie and say that someone saw him or her at the scene of the crime. That usually makes the suspect tell everything."

Good advice. I wished I could use it to find out what Joey was hiding about Lily.

· 6 ·

The Secret in the Closet

Joey and Maxine crossed Russell Street together, leaving me in front of Bud's corner store. The way Joey bounced and jumped, I could tell he was singing one of his songs. It looked as though he was at the "Oh, baby, baby" part.

Maxine took long, forceful steps and her back was so straight the only things that bounced were her curls. Joey kept up with her until he tripped. As he desperately flung his arms to save himself, she looked at him as if she was thinking, "I don't *believe* Maria actually likes this—"

"Hey, if it isn't the Amazing Valvano. How's tricks?"

Ernie had driven up to make his afternoon delivery. I looked back across the street. Joey was running up East Culver to Lily's and Maxine was on Russell, headed toward her house.

"I hope your magic act's all set." Ernie got out of his truck and opened the back door. "I can't wait to see you in the show. I'm even having my hair styled by Maxine's mom next Tuesday."

Tears filled my eyes.

"Jeez, what's the matter? I didn't mean to upset you." He handed me a tissue. "What's all this about?"

I told him everything.

"Jeez, what a shame. To think someone would do a rotten thing like that. Your mom must be furious."

"She doesn't know yet. Please don't tell her. She thinks Lester just escaped in our apartment. I promised to stay out of trouble until Dad gets back. If he were here the kidnapper wouldn't have dared come into our house."

"You know something?" Ernie said. "I saw that Reggie kid near your front door this morning when I dropped off my first delivery. He was standing by the mailbox. He's bad news. I caught him and Kevin stealing bread from my truck last month."

"Thanks, Ernie. I'll follow up on that. You might be a key witness."

"Hey, nothing to it. I hope you find Lester." He gave me a thumbs-up sign for good luck as I ran down the street.

Mary Louise answered her front door and said, "Go away, Maria. You can't come in now. I'm busy."

"I'm doing an article for the school newspaper. I only have a few questions and they're very important."

"You'll have to ask someone else."

Her face was scrunched up and sunlight glinted off her braces. She looked as if she wished I'd disappear. If she could read my mind she'd know I felt the same way about her.

"The article's on the smartest girls in our class." Now she looked interested. "But if you don't want to be in it, I'll understand."

She opened the door and said, "All right, all right. Come in, but only for five minutes."

"No. You have a right to your privacy. I don't want to bother you."

"Maria Valvano, you'd better ask me those questions right now. After all, I am the most intelligent girl in our class."

I really did write for the school newspaper. I was sure an article like the one I was describing would be printed.

"Some of these questions are kind of private. Could we go into your bedroom?"

"No. Nobody's home but me. You can ask me right here."

I had to get into her bedroom to search for Lester. "I have to describe what the smartest girls' living arrangements are like: where they sleep, where they study — things like that."

"I said no, so get on with it."

Most adults thought Mary Louise was charming. I wished I were tape-recording our talk so people would know what she was really like.

The phone rang and Mary Louise went into the kitchen to answer it. This was a lucky break. I ran to her room and looked around. Pale pink curtains waved dreamily over a spotless and wrinkleless bedspread. But no Lester — not a trace, not even a piece of shredded newspaper or a prop from the magic act. Nothing was out of place in the pink-and-white-ruffled bedroom.

I sniffed hard but couldn't detect Lester's smell. All I could smell was wild strawberry, Mary Louise's favorite perfume. She had it in soap, powder, lotion, and sachet.

I worked fast — first scanning her desk — but found nothing. I rifled through three stacks of papers, two notebooks, and six drawers. Nothing. I got down and looked under her bed. Still nothing, and I could hear her yelling down the hall, "Maria Valvano, you get out of my bedroom."

Then I spotted her closet. Of course, she probably hid Lester in there. I headed for the door, but she ran into her room and stopped me.

"What do you think you're doing?" Even after running, Mary Louise's curly blond hair fell perfectly in place.

"I told you. I'm doing a special article for the school

newspaper on the smartest girls in our class."

"I don't believe you. You're up to something and I'm sure it has to do with that Lester."

"Why are you so sure?" I looked at her eyes, in hopes they'd waver as proof she was lying. But they didn't waver once while she answered, "Because you only do things that involve him. I see you going over to Joey's every day. I know you're playing with Lester."

"If you're so smart, where were you and Lily Nakamura going this afternoon with that big bag?"

"To our tap class. We're going to win the talent show — not you. What's going on?"

I didn't want to tell her, not until I'd looked in her closet. Maybe she had gone to a tap class that afternoon. Then again, maybe not. Mary Louise would lie to win the show.

"Why can't I look in your closet?"

"Because you can't, that's why. Now you'd better go or I'm telling your mother."

She would tell my mother. Mary Louise told on everyone.

"Okay, okay. Don't get excited." I headed to the front door.

"Hey!" she yelled after me. "What about the questions? You can't leave me out of the article."

"Can I look into your closet?"

"No."

"Call me when you change your mind."

"You're going to be sorry if you leave me out of the article. I'll tell your mother. I'll tell Sister Margaret. I'll even tell the principal."

I let the apartment door slam on her words. She could tell the world if she wanted to. But while she was telling, I was going to look in her closet.

· 7 ·

The Bump in the Backpack

My house was on the corner of East Culver and Russell streets. East Culver was long, with a bend in the middle and lots of trees. It went from Grove to Washington. And except for the corner store I lived over, there were only apartment buildings and houses on it.

I had thirty minutes left before meeting Maxine and Joey, so I stood across the street from my house and took notes. All the suspects lived near me. Mary Louise and Lily lived down East Culver toward Grove. Reggie lived up East Culver toward Washington, just past Mrs. Bossi's house with the flower garden in front.

Kevin and Maxine lived on Russell near Culver. Further down Russell was Joey's house.

Curiously, at that very moment Kevin was crossing Russell Street. I ducked behind a tree. He was walking with his shoulders hunched forward, his hands in his pockets. He kept looking around as if he knew he was being watched.

He tried my front door. When it didn't open, he rang all the bells and ran up the street. That's when I noticed his backpack had a huge bump in it.

A girl jumped into my doorway. After a moment, she crouched behind a parked car. She had on a Saint Anne's uniform: blue plaid skirt, white blouse, green jacket, blue backpack, green kneesocks, and white sneakers. She was tall and thin and was wearing a blue ski mask with holes for her eyes and mouth.

It was Maxine — tailing Kevin!

She hid behind a tree, paused in the alley, then flattened herself out on the side of a house. I joined in, darting from cover to cover. Our threesome continued up East Culver, past Mrs. Bossi's house, past Reggie's, to Washington Street.

Kevin spotted Maxine in the crosswalk. He waved his fists, which were covered with some kind of dark crud. "I know that's you behind that stupid mask, Maxine. Go home or you'll be sorry. And you bug off too, Maria. I see you behind that newspaper stand."

"I won't go home," said Maxine, "until you give Lester to me."

So that bump in Kevin's backpack must be Lester! "Give him back," I shouted. "Right now."

"You asked for this," said Kevin. He pulled Maxine's backpack off her and dumped the contents on the ground. Pencils and papers scattered everywhere. He kicked her notebook into the gutter, then ran up the street yelling, "Get off my case or you'll really be sorry."

I ran after him while Maxine picked up her stuff.

Kevin ran into the empty lot by the juice bar, pulled himself onto the dumpster, and climbed over the wooden fence to Mr. Clark's back yard. "Quit following me."

"No way. Not unless you give Lester back."

"Don't blame me because you lost your stupid rat." He waved a dirty fist at me, then jumped down into the yard.

I pulled myself up on top of the dumpster and almost passed out from the smell of rotting orange peels. I grabbed the fence to keep from sinking. I climbed over and dropped into the yard.

Kevin ran through the lawn furniture, knocking over the barbecue grill. That made Mr. Clark's German shepherd Fang bark his head off on the back porch. Kevin ran for the gate. Fang jumped over the porch railing and chased him. I had second thoughts about chasing Kevin, but it was too late to turn back. I was stuck in the middle of the yard.

Just before the gate, Fang caught up to Kevin and lunged for his leg, clamping his jaws on Kevin's ankle. Kevin let out an unearthly scream and kicked Fang off. As he climbed over the gate, he waved his dirty fist in one last disgusting gesture to me. "I'll get you for this, Maria."

Fang continued to jump up, snarling and barking. I tried to run back to the fence before he noticed me. I made it to the chaise longue when Fang stopped barking. One quick look over my shoulder and I saw he was after me. My sneakers slipped on the wet grass. I prayed to Saint Francis to calm Fang; I didn't want to die being eaten by a dog.

"Nice doggie," I yelled. "Nice, nice doggie. Good boy."

"Faster, Maria, you can make it," yelled Maxine. She was standing on the dumpster, reaching over the fence to me.

Fang panted behind me, gaining with every second.

"Hurry, Maria. Down, big fellow. Down, boy. Go home. Down."

I got to the fence and hurled myself toward the top. Maxine grabbed at my arms and pulled me up just as Fang crashed into the fence. But I was too heavy for her to pull all the way to the top and I couldn't get a handhold anywhere.

I slowly slipped down. One more inch and Fang would have me. He was barking and snapping at my bottom. I could hear someone screaming. It was me. I fell with a thud to the ground. My last words were, "Dear God, take me but let Maxine find Lester."

I covered my face with my hands and tensed while I

waited for Fang to bite. I was sure I felt his saliva dripping on my arm. When nothing happened, I opened my eyes. Fang was whimpering.

"Sit, Fang. Stay," yelled a deep voice. "What are you kids doing? Haven't you learned that Fang's a watchdog?" Mr. Clark helped me up. "Aren't you a little young to be chasing boys?"

"No — I mean, I wasn't — I mean . . ."

"Forget it. Nothing's broken." While Fang barked and growled, Mr. Clark lifted me to the top of the fence. "Don't come back. I might not be here to save you next time."

· 8 ·

The Mysterious Smell

"I can't believe I was almost killed by a dog for a bump in Kevin's backpack." I leaned against the dumpster and brushed dirt off my skirt. "Why didn't you say something?"

Maxine shrugged. "When? And who knows what was in Kevin's backpack? When I asked where he was this afternoon, he refused to tell me anything. He banged things around his room and left." She pulled an orange peel off my kneesock. "Let's go to my parents' shop. Maybe we'll find out something there."

The beauty shop was one block up Washington. On the way, I told Maxine what I'd learned from Ernie and Mary Louise.

"We have to find out what she's hiding in her closet," said Maxine, writing in her notebook.

We were silent for a moment; then I said, "You know, we could go tonight. Mary Louise's going to the slide show at the church auditorium with her parents. My mom's going, too."

"How would we get in?"

"I know where Mary Louise's spare key is." One thing about our neighborhood: we all knew where everyone's spare key was hidden.

"But — but — that's against the law," whispered Maxine.

"Not if Lester's in her closet."

"But you don't have any proof."

"I'm sure Lester's there. I'm sure of it."

"What if we get caught?" asked Maxine. "We could go to jail."

"We're not going to get caught."

Maxine shook her head. "We need a search warrant."

"We don't have time to get a search warrant. We have to find Lester as soon as possible."

"I'll look it up in my guide." Maxine took off her backpack. "Hey, wait a minute. We can't go tonight. My dad's staying home. There's no way I can sneak out."

"I'll go alone. I can be in and out without anyone knowing."

"Wait for me. You don't know what detectives are supposed to do," said Maxine.

"Yes, I do."

"Maria, we'll talk about this later. Sometimes you are so . . ."

I pushed open the door to Evalina's Beauty Affair and forgot everything else. I loved this shop. If I weren't going to be a magician, I'd work here.

There were wonderfully strong, flowery smells that I wished I could smell all the time. And there were zebra-striped chairs and leopard-skin smocks that I'd give anything to have at home, but Mom said no whenever I asked.

Mrs. McCollem was plucking a woman's eyebrows. "Hi, girls. Why do you have on that ski mask, Maxine?"

"It's a disguise, Mom. Have you seen Kevin?"

"He was here earlier this afternoon. Take the mask off. It looks ridiculous."

"How long was he here?" I asked.

"From twelve-thirty to two-thirty. He unpacked shampoo and conditioners. I think he's turning over a new leaf."

Maxine gave me a look and whispered, "Give me a break."

"Your haircut looks good, Maria. Do you still like it?"

"Oh, yes, Mrs. McCollem."

"How are your mother's driving lessons coming along?"

"Fine except for parallel parking. She keeps landing on the sidewalk."

Several customers laughed. A few pretended they were reading magazines.

"It's not a good idea to tell family secrets," said Mrs. McCollem.

Maxine came to my rescue and pulled me down the hall. "We're going to check the back room, then go to Maria's house, Mom."

"Okay, dear, but change your uniform before you play. I think your mother would want you to do the same, Maria."

"You have to admit he had time to kidnap Lester," said Maxine as we walked past two stone sinks to the back room.

"What's that smell?" I asked.

Maxine wrinkled her nose and looked at the metal shelves filled with conditioners, shampoos, dyes, and permanents. "I don't know. Maybe Kevin broke a bottle back here."

"Or maybe he washed his hair."

"C'mon. He'd wash his shoes first."

Maxine wrote *mysterious smell* in her notebook, then turned on all the lights. We searched everywhere but didn't find a trace of Lester. All we found was Kevin's usual pile of garbage — crumpled cans of sour cherry soda and an empty bag of beef jerky.

"I guess we can't cross Kevin off the list of suspects," I said. "But I have my doubts — there wasn't any evidence here or at your house. Besides, I'm sure Mary Louise is the kidnapper."

"Let's find out what Joey's discovered."

"Okay. But we have to talk more about tonight. One of us has to go to Mary Louise's. Lester's life might depend on it."

· 9 ·

The Break-in Plan

"Reggie did it," said Joey, leaning against my front door with a look of triumph on his face.

Reggie? I'd forgotten about Reggie, and besides, I was sure Mary Louise was the kidnapper. I didn't want to hear that it was Reggie. I wanted to hear more evidence for my suspect.

Joey continued. "Reggie said he was at the arcade since school got out, but I knew he was lying because his eyes kept wavering — just like you said, Maxine — and when I checked with the manager he said Reggie didn't get there until after three-thirty."

I had to tell Joey: "Ernie saw him by my doorway this morning."

"Aha! He was probably casing your place. After I left the arcade I went to his house and found this on his front porch." He held up a pad of paper.

"Oh, Joey," said Maxine, "that was brave of you." From the sound of her voice I knew she was impressed.

"It doesn't have anything on it," I said, making sure the front door locked before we went upstairs to my apartment.

"It's the same kind of paper the drawing of the hooded rat was on."

"Anybody could have this kind of paper," I protested.

"Detectives have to note everything," said Maxine, adding the information to the suspect chart and her notebook.

"What about Lily?" she asked. "We have more on everyone but her."

"She's okay," said Joey, blushing.

"Okay?" I exclaimed. "How about guilty or not guilty?"

"Not guilty," he said, and Maxine wrote NOT GUILTY on the chart under Lily's name. "She was sorry to hear about Lester."

"I bet. Why did you tell her about the kidnapping? By now everyone probably knows." I drew a big question mark under the NOT GUILTY.

"Who said we couldn't tell anyone?" asked Joey.

"Yeah. Why not?" asked Maxine. "I told Kevin — didn't you tell Mary Louise?"

"No, and I don't think Lily —"

"Look, Maria," said Joey. "Lester's my rat. I can do what I want. You're not the boss."

Maxine stared at me. "Yeah. And by the way, *I'm* in charge of the suspect chart — that means *I* write on it."

"Boy, you guys sure are touchy today."

"For your information," said Joey, "Lily and Mary Louise went to a tap class this afternoon to work on their act for the show."

"Did her eyes waver?"

"Cut it out, Maria. After the class she went home to do her homework and so did Mary Louise because they're going to the slide show on Italy tonight."

I couldn't prove Joey was wrong about Lily and I didn't want him and Maxine to get any angrier with me. "Sorry. I'm just worried about Lester — I don't want a suspect to get away too fast."

"Who's getting away fast?" asked Maxine. "So far everyone but Lily looks guilty. We have to eliminate suspects sometime."

"I guess so." I wasn't convinced, but since I wanted to go to Mary Louise's that night, I decided to stop talking about Lily.

I told Joey what had happened at Mary Louise's and my plan to go to her house. "Want to go with me tonight?"

"But that's illegal! That's breaking and entering!"

"Detectives can do that. Can't they, Maxine?"

Maxine was flipping the pages of her detective's guide. "Funny, it doesn't say anything about that at all. It just says what to do when you search someone's place. But I don't think *we* can go into someone's house. We're not really detectives."

"Oh, Maxine, you're so — so picky. Look, you guys. We're just going to run in and get Lester and run out."

"I don't know," said Joey.

"I think you should wait for me," said Maxine.

"Look, you guys discuss it. I just have one thing more to say. If one of you were in Mary Louise's closet, I'd come and get you."

While they talked, I went to the kitchen to put the lasagna in the oven. I heard Maxine say, "She always . . . thinks she knows more than . . . maybe you'd . . . call me if . . . be careful."

When I returned, Joey said, "I'm going. Lester's my rat. Let's meet at seven-thirty by the gate in Mary Louise's back yard. We'll go in, get Lester, and come right back out."

"Fine," I agreed.

"It's not fine," said Maxine. "It's —"

"Let's not start this argument all over again," said Joey.

"My mom will be home soon. We have to clean up this mess."

"Can't we leave it this way?" asked Maxine. "The basic detective rule is: protect the scene of the crime. This room is supposed to be off-limits to anyone except those processing it for evidence."

"No. Mom told me to find Lester and bring him back to Joey's. That's what she'll think I've done. She doesn't know about the kidnapping. I was going to tell her but now I'm not because she'll blame me for someone breaking into our house. She'll ground me, call the police—"

"Enough," said Maxine. "We'll go with the evidence we've found. But don't blame me if we lose something important."

While we cleaned, Maxine read from her guide about how to search someone's place: "Bring a flashlight. Don't turn on any lights until you've closed the blinds. Walk softly so you don't tip off neighbors. Wear black."

Joey rolled his eyes.

"Okay, okay," I said. "I'll wear my black pants, Dad's black sweat shirt, Mom's black sneakers."

"Good. Good," she said.

Before she left she gave me her ski mask. "Use this to cover your face. Don't take it off."

Five minutes later she came back. "Wear these." She gave me a pair of plastic gloves.

I was getting my clothes ready when the phone rang.

"Don't forget to put Mary Louise's key back."

"I won't. I won't."

"And one more thing."

"What?" I shouted. I was ready to burn her detective's guide.

"Good luck."

· 10 ·

An Exciting Escape

"What a lesson!" said Mom. "Today I learned to stop and start a car on a hill. I even turned around on a hill." She threw her coat and purse on my bed. "I'm still having trouble with parallel parking, but Mr. Anson says I'm doing just fine. I bet you can't wait for me to drive you around."

"I don't know. It depends . . ."

"Maria, you're going to love it. My driving will change our life."

Whenever she said those words, they meant disaster.

"Oops, I'd better hurry dinner. Mrs. Bossi is giving me a ride to the slide show at seven o'clock. Want to come with us?" She gathered up her things.

"I have too much homework."

"That's too bad. Maybe next time."

She went to the kitchen, humming and singing. I sat on my chair, moaning and sighing.

After dinner she put a tin of brownies on the table. "Get to bed early. I'll tell you all about the slide show tomorrow."

"Okay, Mom. Have a good time."

I knew I would. Nothing was more satisfying than getting even with Mary Louise.

I was confident people couldn't recognize me in my black clothes and Maxine's ski mask, but to be safe I stayed close to buildings and crouched when I walked under the street lights. Joey was waiting for me by Mary Louise's gate as planned.

"They left twenty minutes ago," he whispered. "We've got the place to ourselves."

I handed him a pair of plastic gloves. "So we don't leave any fingerprints."

He held up his hands encased in plastic gloves. "Too late. Maxine already got to me."

We tiptoed up the back steps to the third floor. I got the spare key from under the birdseed on the deck, unlocked the door to Mary Louise's kitchen, then returned the key.

I used my flashlight to guide Joey to her room. He closed the blinds and I turned on the lamp by her bed.

"Dang," he said. "This is incredible. Everything's pink." He touched the ruffles. "These are . . . beautiful." He sniffed the air. "The room smells good. It's . . . it's—"

"Wild strawberry." I couldn't believe Joey liked her room.

He played with her three-way mirror. "Hey, I can see the back of my head."

"All I want to see is the back of her closet." But the phone rang and I froze. "What should we do?"

"Don't answer it," said Joey. "We'd give ourselves away."

The phone kept ringing.

"What if it's Maxine, trying to warn us about something?"

The phone kept ringing. Each ring jangled my stomach.

"I can't stand it any longer." I held the phone so that Joey and I could both listen. But whoever it was hung up.

"Weird," said Joey.

I rubbed sweat from my hands and walked across the room. At last I was going to find out the secret of Mary Louise's closet. I yanked open the door.

Nothing.

Well, not exactly nothing. There were more dresses than I'd ever seen in a closet. Most of them pink. There were also pants, blouses, skirts, belts, scarves, and sweaters, all hung carefully by color. Six pairs of shoes hung in a pink vinyl shoe bag on the door. There was even a long pink velour bathrobe. But no Lester.

"Where is he?" I shouted, pushing the clothes aside.

"She has more clothes than my mother," said Joey.

"Mine too. You know she'd never put Lester in here. He'd smell up her clothes."

"Dang. That's just great. We break the law and Lester isn't even here. I wonder why she wouldn't let you look in her closet."

"Who knows. Let's search the room."

Joey started on her desk and I tackled her bureau. Three drawers later I found the Wonder Woman pajamas that she'd blackmailed out of me a month ago.

"I'm taking these back."

"You can't. She'd know you were here."

I hated to admit it but he was right.

After twenty minutes Joey looked at his watch and said, "Let's leave. Lester's not here. It's after eight — over five hours since he was kidnapped. We could be investigating another suspect."

"Let's search the rest of the house first."

"Are you kidding?"

"As long as we're here. Look, she could have moved him so her mother wouldn't find him."

We were walking down the hall when we heard the front door unlock. We scrambled back into Mary Louise's bedroom.

"Take her into the bathroom," said Mr. O'Brien. "She'll be okay."

Joey and I hid in Mary Louise's closet and squished ourselves behind the dresses.

The bathroom was next to Mary Louise's room. We heard gagging and Mrs. O'Brien saying, "That's what happens when you . . . candy and popcorn on top of . . . no wonder . . ." When Mary Louise threw up, Joey and I giggled. I was glad she was sick, but I wished she'd waited till we were gone.

Someone came into the room and opened the closet door. I held my breath. Joey trembled next to me. The long pink robe was pulled off its hook. When the closet door closed, I slumped onto the floor.

"I prayed the whole time," whispered Joey.

"Don't stop. We're not out of here yet."

"I'm scared."

"Me too."

In case Mary Louise needed her slippers I pushed them up against the door.

Mary Louise was in the bedroom now. I had to put my hand over my mouth to keep from giggling and Joey couldn't stop snorting until Mr. O'Brien said, "Good night, Mary Louise. Let this be a lesson to you."

"Now what?" whispered Joey in my ear.

I had to take Maxine's ski mask off so I could hear. "We're stuck in here until she goes to sleep," I whispered in his ear.

"Oh, no," said Joey. "We could be here all night."

"I hope not. I've got to be back before Mom."

We sat quietly for what seemed to be forever. I felt hot and itchy, and my left foot was falling asleep. I moved, but couldn't get comfortable. Joey was shifting around, too.

"I can't stand it in here any more," he said.

"Keep your voice down," I whispered. "If she finds us, our lives are over — done for — finished." I shuddered at what could happen to us.

"I don't feel good. That smell in here. It's getting to me. I . . ."

"Joey, please." I rubbed his back. His neck felt cold and damp. He couldn't be sick. He just couldn't. "Think thoughts of being well. Think about running in the park, swimming."

Joey moaned and slumped against the wall.

"Maybe we should run for the back door," I said, pulling him up onto his knees. "We'll duck our heads so Mary Louise can't see our faces. It might work."

Joey gagged.

I tried to push his head to his knees, but he fell forward on his forehead with a thud. I froze, afraid that Mary Louise had heard us, but she was snoring.

I shook Joey. "She's asleep. We can escape. Hang on." I opened the door and let Joey breathe some fresh air while I watched Mary Louise's nose quiver.

"I'm okay now," whispered Joey. "Let's go."

He didn't sound okay, but we had to go.

In the pink glow of the ballerina night-light, we crawled out of the closet, across the room, and into the hall, trying not to laugh out loud when Mary Louise snored. We tiptoed down the hall, past the living room where Mr. and Mrs. O'Brien were watching television. We continued into the kitchen and were almost to the door when Joey bumped into a chair.

"Ow!" he cried. "Ow! My knee."

"Shh! Wait till we're outside." I pulled open the door. It opened more easily than I expected and banged against the counter.

"Who's that? Who's in there?" yelled Mr. O'Brien, coming out of the living room and turning on lights. "Call the police, Kate."

Mrs. O'Brien screamed.

"What's going on?" yelled Mary Louise. "It's impossible to sleep around here."

I pushed Joey outside. We tripped and ran down the stairs, making it out the bottom door before the first-floor neighbor came out to the landing.

We ran through the back yard and climbed over the fence.

"I told you this was dangerous and illegal," said Joey, rubbing his knee.

"I didn't think it would be *this* dangerous."

We could still hear Mr. O'Brien yelling. In the distance were sirens.

"Oh, no. The police are coming," I said. "I can't get caught. My mom's captain of the neighborhood crime-watch."

"Then we'd better get home before the police get here." Joey took off through the back yards to his house and I ran down the alley to Russell Street. I jumped in and out of doorways to the corner. I waited for a few cars to pass, then ran across the street to my back yard, getting inside the gate just as a police car arrived.

I raced upstairs, tore off my clothes, and stuffed them under the bed. I looked out the window and saw more police cars with flashing lights and a crowd of people in front of Mary Louise's. I couldn't go to sleep: I'd barely escaped going to jail and I hadn't found Lester. Where was he? Who had him? Did the kidnapper know what Lester liked to eat? Or that Lester took a long time to try new foods?

I was still worrying about Lester when Mom came home. "What are you doing up?" she asked.

"The sirens woke me. What happened?"

"Someone broke into the O'Briens' apartment. Everyone's okay. You'll find out about it in the morning. We're going to have to increase our neighborhood security.

We're having a special meeting of the neighborhood crime-watch tomorrow."

"Mom, I don't think we should hide our key in the hall anymore. Anyone could take it and break into our apartment and —"

Mom brushed the hair off my forehead. "Good idea. I'll get the key right now. We'll leave it with Bud. Go to sleep. Everything will be all right."

If only that were true.

· 11 ·

The Competition

"You're lucky you weren't caught," said Maxine, as she helped carry what was left of the magic act props to school. "You caused so much excitement my dad even left his favorite television program to find out what was happening."

"I'll never do that again. Do you know there were four police cars?"

"All it takes is one to catch you."

"We didn't find any clues. I'm baffled."

"Mary Louise isn't dumb. She probably moved Lester after she talked to you."

"We can't tell anyone. If my mom finds out she'll kill me."

"You can trust me," said Maxine. "But I don't know about Joey."

"I trust him . . . except —"

"Except?" Maxine opened her notebook and wrote *The Trouble with Joey*.

"Except where Lily is concerned. Like last night — he defends her too much. And then while I was trying to go to sleep I had this crazy thought — what if Joey kidnapped Lester?"

"Now that *is* crazy. He owns Lester."

"True." I shifted the trick box to my other hip. "But you know how he feels about Lily. Do you think I should investigate her myself?"

"She's not the kidnapper type. A kidnapper has to be desperate, like my brother. I'm sure he did it. You know how you can just know something?"

"Yeah, like I'm sure Mary Louise did it and Joey's sure Reggie did it. But something else: last night the phone rang at Mary Louise's. It wasn't you, was it?"

"No. Why would I do that?"

"To warn me or remind me to look for something. Funny, I was sure the call was for me. Some things you just don't know the answer to."

Mary Louise was telling everyone in the school yard what had happened at her house. "My dad scared them off before they could take anything. My dad used to be in the Marines. There were three or four robbers — at least three. They could have had guns. But my dad and I showed them. We didn't give them a chance to get out of the kitchen."

"Boy, Mary Louise, you're tough," said Wayne Wong.

"I would have jumped in my closet," said Najuma Jefferson.

"I bet you were scared, girl," sneered Reggie.

"No, I was right beside my dad." Mary Louise stuck her chest out. "I had the pipe from the vacuum cleaner, so I was ready for anything."

I gave Maxine a meaningful look.

"How did they get in?" asked Lily.

"With a master key, like spies have. We're going to get new locks with dead bolts. Chains, too." She answered questions till the bell rang and we filed into school.

Sister Margaret was pushing a table to the back of the classroom. "Leave your props for the talent show here. I'll screen the acts after recess."

I put our props on the table. Ernie had lent us his magic rings and hat. Maxine had found us all black capes.

Sister Margaret ran her fingers along the teeth of my saw. "My, my. I don't like the looks of this."

I wrote *The Amazing Valvano* on a sheet of paper and put it on top of my props.

"You're amazing, all right," she said.

We spent the morning reviewing math. When Lily went to the board to demonstrate percentages, I watched

Joey watching her. I didn't like her even if she was innocent.

Reggie went after Lily. On his way back to his seat, he pinched me and everyone in my row.

At recess no one played ball or jumped rope. Mary Louise told her story, which got longer and longer.

"Pretty soon she'll be telling people she beat off the intruders herself and saved her mother and father," I said.

Reggie and Wayne spit at us from the top of the jungle gym.

"Forget them," said Maxine. "Anything else on the act?"

"Get a question from Sister Margaret and give it to me last."

"What about the first question?" asked Joey.

"I'll guess at it today. The night of the show, Ernie will ask the first question and I'll know the answer."

After recess Sister Margaret marked off a stage area at the front of the classroom. "Okay, Reggie. Let's see your stuff."

Reggie juggled three red balls, but kept dropping them. "Don't worry," he said. "I'm going to practice all weekend."

"Try praying," said Sister Margaret.

Reggie changed to bowling pins, throwing them high in the air. They hit the floor with a thwack and bounced.

"Man, you are not the greatest," said Najuma as she and Sylvie Boland moved out of their seats.

"Enough," shouted Sister Margaret. "You'll kill someone."

"I'll be careful," he said, but a pin skidded across the floor into her chair. She hopped up. "This act is out, out."

"Wait — you haven't seen the flaming torches."

"Flaming torches?"

Reggie held up three sticks. "I light the ends. Want to see?"

"No. Absolutely no flaming torches, balls, or pins. Next, please."

Najuma got up to play her flute.

Sister Margaret sat down and fanned herself with a piece of paper.

Reggie grumbled, "Man, that music will never be on the charts."

Three acts later, Mary Louise and Lily posed at each end of the stage. When the music began, they tap-danced toward each other. They turned, twisted, stamped, and shuffled, making wonderful sounds.

"Nice, very nice," said Sister Margaret, clapping along with the music.

I hated to admit they were good, but they were, especially Mary Louise. She was smooth. She was exciting. And she made me hate her more than ever before. It wasn't fair that she could do so many things better than I could.

My only consolation was that her mouth hung open while she danced. It truly did. Her lower jaw hung loose and wobbled. It stayed that way, looking dumb, all the way through her dance.

"We do four time-steps in this number," she explained. "A single, a double, a triple, and a double triple. We end with a triple time-step break which is *very* difficult. We're going to wear hot pink leotards, fishnet —"

"That's enough, Mary Louise," said Sister Margaret, turning to me. "Okay, Maria, you're next. I can't wait to see the Amazing Valvano."

· 12 ·

An Incredible Magic Trick

Maxine separated and joined the magic metal rings while Joey and I did scarf tricks. When we pulled paper flowers from our mouths, kids clapped and yelled.

"The Amazing Valvano will now perform mental telepathy," announced Joey.

I stood in the middle of the stage area, pretending to go into a trance while he and Maxine collected questions and answers.

The first question was from Sylvie Boland. "How old is my grandmother's dog?"

I acted as if I were thinking hard. "The answer is fuzzy. It's having a hard time coming through."

Kids giggled.

"Her brain is fuzzy," said Mary Louise.

"Quiet, class," said Sister Margaret.

I waved an envelope in front of my face. "Eighteen," I guessed.

"She's right," said Sylvie, looking surprised.

"Wow," said John Rice. "Do my question next."

I opened the envelope as if to verify Sylvie's answer and read the answer to the next question so that when Joey asked, "What color tie did John's father wear this morning?" I already knew the answer.

I folded my arms, closed my eyes, and counted to five. "I see red whales on a gray background."

"Hey! She's right," said John.

"How did she do that?" asked Najuma.

"Yeah, how?" asked others.

With each question, I expanded the way I thought of the answer: putting fingers on my forehead, closing my eyes, humming. By the time I got to Sister Margaret's question, my thinking took almost a minute.

Her question was: "What saint's medal do I have in my pocket?"

I raised my arms and bowed to the left, then to the right. Facing straight ahead, I hummed and lowered my arms until they were almost at my sides. I began to twirl — slowly at first, then faster and faster.

Now Sister Margaret would know I could do something great. So would Mary Louise. I twirled until I felt dizzy. "I see a man on a hillside — he's throwing stones — no — he's feeding, feeding — animals. It's Saint Francis — Saint Francis of Assisi!"

Sister Margaret jumped up, putting her hand on her

chest. "I don't believe it — this is incredible. How did you do it?"

"It's a miracle," whispered Maxine.

The class cheered.

"I bet they cheated," said Reggie.

"Me too," said Mary Louise.

I silenced the class with: "The night of the show I'm going to saw a rabbit in half." I held up my teddy bear. "Today I'm sawing this bear."

The class cheered again.

"You must bring the rabbit to the audition next Wednesday," said Sister Margaret.

I put the teddy bear in the box. While I tightened the straps, Joey was supposed to open the secret panel in back, remove the teddy bear from the box, and put him in the magician's hat that Maxine was holding behind the table out of sight of the audience.

"The panel's stuck," he whispered. "I can't get him out."

"What'll we do?" Maxine forced a smile.

"Just get him out of the way of the saw." I put the top of the box on, snapped the locks shut, and continued tightening straps to stall for time.

"Having trouble?" asked Sister Margaret.

"No. Everything's fine."

Joey whispered, "This is the best I can do. Let's give it a try."

I inserted the saw and pretended it took all my strength to saw through the teddy bear when actually I was sawing through a black sponge on the bottom of the box. The sawing made a sickening sound, as if I were ripping through flesh.

Some kids held their breath. Others looked nervous. I heard whispers. The whispers became murmurs. The kids in front shouted, "Oh, no." "Help!"

Maxine put her hand on my arm. "Stuffing's falling out of the box."

I looked down. A slow, steady stream of stuffing trickled onto the floor. I undid the locks and yanked off the box cover. What I saw made me put my hand over my mouth.

"Yuck," said Sylvie.

"I'm going to be sick," said Mary Louise.

"Maria killed the bear. Maria killed the bear," chanted Reggie and his friends Wayne, Christian, and Jesse.

The teddy bear's left leg fell to the floor with a dull thud. Stuffing continued to flow from his torso onto the floor, pooling around the crumpled limb.

Some kids ran toward me. Others jumped up on their chairs. Reggie made throw-up sounds and laughed.

"Back. Back to your seats," shouted Sister Margaret. She grabbed the teddy bear's remains and said, "Maria Valvano, wait for me in the hall."

· 13 ·

An Assignment for
Monday Morning

While Joey and Maxine cleaned up the stuffing, Sister Margaret got everyone settled down with a silent reading assignment and joined me in the hall.

"No matter what you do, you cause trouble. Why?"

I couldn't think of anything to say.

"What was going through your head when you mutilated this animal? Well? Speak."

"It was an accident, Sister. It won't happen in the show. Honest."

"You expect me to believe you and have you kill a real rabbit at the audition?"

"He won't be in the box when I'm sawing. The secret panel got stuck and we couldn't get the teddy bear out of the way of the saw. Please, Sister Margaret. You liked the first part of our act."

"It has potential."

She opened the classroom door. "If you can't stay in your seat now, Reggie, you'll have to stay in it after school." She turned back to me. "Are you sure you can fix the box?"

"Yes, Sister. I promise."

"Goodness only knows why I'm giving you another chance, because I certainly don't. Listen carefully, Maria. The first part of your act is good. I don't know how you do it, but I know a winning act when I see one. If you can get your act working by next Wednesday's audition, you're in the show. Otherwise you're part of the tech crew. Is that clear?"

"Yes, Sister. Thank you, Sister."

Sister Margaret took the class down to lunch. She told Maxine, Joey, and me to finish cleaning up. Reggie and Wayne lip-synched her words and Mary Louise smirked. The rest of the kids stared at us.

"We really blew it," I said, slumping down in my chair.

"Just when we were doing great," said Maxine, packing up our props. "Sister Margaret was impressed. Did you see her face when you answered her question?"

"I wish I had a picture." All I had was a paper bag with the teddy bear's remains.

"I told you we shouldn't use the bear," said Joey, "but you —"

"The bear was fine. It was the panel that got stuck."

"It wasn't my fault," yelled Joey.

"It wasn't mine either."

"Hey, guys," said Maxine. "It wasn't anybody's fault. We have to stick together. Remember? Our big problem is the audition. Sister Margaret wants us to bring a rabbit."

"Don't worry about a rabbit. We're going to find Lester." I banged the broom for emphasis.

"Have it your way. What's our game plan?" asked Joey.

"We'll each follow a suspect after school," said Maxine. "And you can't come home without a clue."

I got Kevin, Maxine got Mary Louise, and Joey got Reggie.

"If we don't find anything, I'm going to offer a reward," said Joey. "I can't stand worrying about Lester. It's been twenty-one hours since he was kidnapped."

"I worry about him, too," I said. "A lot. But let's wait another day before offering a reward. I want the kidnapper to wonder what we're doing. And I haven't told my mom yet."

"Let her think Lester was kidnapped from my house," said Joey. "Whoever says he wasn't is the kidnapper. I didn't tell anyone where he was kidnapped."

"Neither did I," said Maxine.

We argued about the reward all the way to lunch.

As I walked into the cafeteria, all eyes were riveted on me. Reggie pointed and shouted, "There she is. The teddy bear killer."

"She'll do anything for attention," said Mary Louise.

"She made me sick," said Leah Heckman.

"You're always sick," said Wayne.

By the time I'd gone through the line, everyone in school knew about my act. Kids from other classes crowded around me as I walked to a table. I got separated from Joey and Maxine.

"Your act's grotesque," said Patrick Thomas, a sixth grader. "I mean, you killed a teddy bear."

"Hey, Rat Breath," said Kevin, bumping my shoulder. "I always said you'd make a lousy magician. Are you going to kill a rabbit at the audition?"

I kept my eyes on my tray but questions kept coming. "Why can't you saw Sister Margaret in half?" "Do you have a license?"

I had just sat down when a voice on the P.A. system said, "Will Maria Valvano please report to the principal's office. I repeat. Will Maria Valvano please report to the principal's office."

Now what? Everyone stared at me as if I'd stolen all the desserts. I practically crawled out of the cafeteria.

Sister Agnes *and* Sister Margaret were waiting for me. Sister Agnes took her time adjusting a crucifix on the wall before she said, "You're a busy girl, Maria Valvano. I hear that in addition to working on a magic act, which I plan to watch at the audition next Wednesday, you're writing an article on the smartest girls in your class."

So that's what this was all about: Mary Louise had told on me. I tried to clear myself: "I was *thinking* about doing an article, but I figured the paper gets many more interesting articles and —"

Sister Margaret stepped forward. "You thought wrong, Miss Know-it-all. You're doing the article. If you'd put half as much effort into your studies as you put into causing trouble, you'd be one of the smartest girls in the class yourself."

"Now, now," said Sister Agnes. "Let's not get upset. I'm sure Maria's willing to fulfill her promises."

"I'm not upset," shouted Sister Margaret, waving her arms. "The article's due on my desk Monday morning."

"Yes, Sister."

"I expect you to include Sylvie Boland, Najuma Jefferson, and Lily Nakamura, as well as Mary Louise O'Brien." She leaned so close I could feel her breath on my face. "In the future, do not tell anyone you're writing an article for the school newspaper until you have my approval. Is that clear?"

"Yes, Sister." I edged toward the door.

"Remember me to your mother," said Sister Agnes.

I was furious as I ran back to the classroom. I didn't have time to write an article. I had to find Lester.

I cornered Mary Louise in the coatroom. "You'll be sorry for telling on me."

"It's your own fault. You should have asked me those questions."

"I'll be over after school. And you'd better have answers ready."

· 14 ·

The Confession of a Smart Girl

"Don't get into an argument with those smart girls," warned Maxine. "You can't afford a detention."

"Yeah," added Joey. "They have a hot line to Sister Margaret."

"C'mon you guys, I can handle them." The looks on their faces said they didn't believe me. They told me to do the interviews and they'd continue the search for Lester.

"It's been twenty-four hours since he was kidnapped," noted Joey.

Sylvie Boland was waiting for me on her front steps. "What happened to your act?" she asked.

"Technical difficulties. They'll be fixed by the audition."

"Did Sister Agnes nail you? I mean, is that why you're doing this article?"

"No. Let's stick to why I'm here. How do you study?"

"Like everyone else. Okay? I mean, I look at the material and keep going over it until I know it. Okay? I mean, what if the night of the show you kill the rabbit? Talk about gross."

"Don't worry. That can't happen." I was trying not to get angry. "Why are you one of the smartest girls in the class?"

"Because I work hard all the time: in class, at break, during lunch. I mean, I don't stop until I understand everything. I ask questions — at home, in school, anywhere. I mean, you'd be surprised who'll answer your questions. Once I asked someone washing his—"

"Uh, that's enough, Sylvie. What's the first thing you do when you get home from school?"

"I'll tell if you tell how you knew the answers in your act. Okay?"

"Sylvie, give me a break. If you want to be in the article, answer my questions and forget the magic act."

"Okay. I mean, don't be so touchy. Like today you're totally weird, Maria. Here's what I do: I organize my homework. I stack notebooks, textbooks, and papers of each subject in a pile with a priority number on top. After I figure out how long each subject needs, I write a time slot next to the priority number. I also make a priority number for long projects, practicing the piano, and walking the dog." She beamed at me as if she'd given the winning answer on a television quiz show.

"Thanks, Sylvie. I mean — you've been a big help."

"I'm glad you didn't die of embarrassment today," said Mary Louise. "I really want to see my name in print." She handed me a thick stack of papers. "Here are my reports and tests. As you can see, I got A's on most of them. On some I got an A+. If I don't get an A, I find out why."

I could just see her whining on Sister Margaret's shoulder when she didn't get an A. "How do you prepare for tests?" I asked her.

"I make two notebooks. I put class notes in one and my questions and answers in the other. Sometimes I think of better tests than Sister Margaret."

I bet she did.

"Let me show you my study center and personal computer."

I followed her down the hall, keeping an eye out for places she could hide Lester.

"We've made our house an environment for learning. We play language cassettes during meals."

She started talking in French. If she had Lester, she'd bore him to death. Dear God, I didn't mean that. Please let Lester be safe. Oh, please.

"What's that?" I pointed to a recessed section of the ceiling.

She ignored me. "These books are newly published but

they look like old editions. See the fancy backs on them? They're called raised spines." She held a book up to my nose.

"Great spines, but what's that on your ceiling?"

"The passage to the attic, but we haven't used it in years. The hole's too small for anyone but me."

"How do you get up there?"

"I — with a ladder." She looked away. "Books like these show a family cares about the mental growth of its members. These books are the hallmarks of a superior mind."

"What do you hate most and like best about school?"

"I hate missing the highest mark by one point, like I did on the history test. Sylvie did better because she visited her grandparents in Ireland, but I'll beat her next time. What I like best is being on top."

I snapped my notebook shut. I'd had enough of the superior mind. "See you in print."

"That's it? Don't you want to know how I memorize?"

"I've got enough."

"You'd better give me good coverage."

"You'll get everything you deserve."

Najuma Jefferson was practicing the flute when I arrived.

"My family can't wait to see me written up in the newspaper. I'll tell you anything you want to know. Go ahead — ask."

"Thanks. Why —"

"Of course they wondered about you after I told them what you did with the teddy bear. I personally have never seen anything so disgusting in my life. I can't wait to see what you do with the rabbit in the audition. But why are you fooling around with animals?"

"Because I —"

"I have better things to do — flute, dance classes, and Sylvie and I just joined the swim team. Why don't you come, too?"

"Maybe — after the talent show. First I have to do this article."

"Why write about the smartest girls? You are not where it's at, Maria. You need an attitude adjustment — fast."

Lily Nakamura had made cookies. She didn't bug me about Lester or my magic act. No question about it, she was nice. And she was pretty. I could see why Joey liked her.

Two desks were pushed together in the corner of her bedroom, with shelves over one and a bulletin board over the other. A calendar was marked with special events and due dates of school projects. On yesterday's slot was written: *2:30 — dance class.*

I pretended I didn't see the calendar. "Where did you and Mary Louise go after school yesterday? Readers want to know how the smartest girls spend their time."

"We went to a tap class." She smiled, took a bite of her cookie, and offered me the plate.

"You got to leave school early. Why?"

"Mary Louise and I had a special class to work on our number for the show. Wait till you see what we've added. We're going to look so professional. Our teacher is quite pleased with us. She said she may use us in her lecture-demonstration series this summer and possibly in the fall. We —"

"That's nice."

Lily was definitely a friend of Mary Louise's. She could go on and on just like Mary Louise.

"Where's your dance studio?"

"On Washington Street, next to the supermarket."

Lily smiled and offered me the cookies again. She was too nice. It made me wonder whether she was hiding something. I decided to try Maxine's suggestion for making a suspect talk. "I heard you really like to dance," I said.

"Oh, yes. I'm planning to be a dancer. Right now I take ballet, jazz, and tap. This summer I'm going to a serious workshop in —"

"Well, if you're serious about dance then you wouldn't want to miss a class, would you?" I took another cookie and smiled at her.

"No."

"And you wouldn't want to be late for a class, either."
She shook her head no. She wasn't smiling now. I felt
I was on to something.

"Then what were you doing in front of my house yesterday afternoon when you were supposed to be at the
dance studio?" I lied.

"How did — uh — uh . . ." Her eyes wavered and she
looked as if she wanted to run away. "I can't say . . ."

I couldn't believe it. I'd hit the jackpot. And there was
more to find out. "Tell me, Lily. You have to." She looked
down at her lap. "You can trust me. Really." I put my
hand on her shoulder. "Where was Mary Louise?"

"On her way home. She forgot her leotard and there's
a dress code at the dance studio — we have to wear black
leotards and tights."

This was incredible news. Did it mean that Mary Louise
was the kidnapper or Lily or both of them?

Lily wrung her hands.

"Sister Margaret expected you to be at that class," I
said, trying to make Lily feel guilty. "She *trusted* you to
be at that class. And if you don't want her to know you
weren't at that class, you'd better tell me everything. You
know, Lily, people can get into big trouble for kidnapping a rat."

Lily's eyes widened and she dropped her cookie.

"I wouldn't consider kidnapping a rat. I'm allergic to
animal hair. And rats are so — so — dirty."

She shivered and almost gagged. I had to admit she was convincing, and yet . . .

"This is pretty serious," I said, looking as concerned as I could.

"Please don't tell," she pleaded. "On the way to Mary Louise's we stopped to buy candy at Bud's. It took a long time, so Mary Louise told me to go to the dance studio before the dance teacher called Saint Anne's to see where we were. I did and Mary Louise came later with her leotard."

"How interesting," I said. "How very, very interesting." I crossed my fingers. "Don't worry, I won't tell Sister Margaret."

And I wouldn't tell her — unless I had to.

· 15 ·

A Horrendous Discovery

"We need to try another approach," said Maxine, looking through her guide. She and Joey had stopped by my place on their way home. "Nancy Drew says to get samples of handwriting, learn fortunetelling, make up a secret code."

"You got samples of handwriting," I said. "They didn't help."

"How about a secret code?" asked Maxine. "I like that. Then we could leave messages for each other. How about it? We could make one up tomorrow."

"Forget the secret code," I said. "We'll never use it."

"I think we should offer a reward," said Joey. "It's been twenty-six and a half hours since Lester was kidnapped and we don't have solid evidence on anyone."

"We have to keep looking for Lester. We don't have time to do all these other things like coming up with a secret code or making reward fliers. Besides, making fliers is difficult."

"No, it isn't," said Joey. "I know what to do. I've helped my mom make a lot of fliers. It's no biggie."

"What about the money? We don't have—"

"Maria, I'm doing the flier." Joey banged his hand on my desk.

"What about what Lily said about Mary Louise?"

"So they didn't do what Sister Margaret expected them to do," said Joey. "You ought to know about that. You do the same thing all the time."

"*Joey!* I thought you were my friend."

"Well, you do. And anyhow, forget about suspecting Lily. She's not guilty. And what she said only proves that Mary Louise was in the neighborhood. It doesn't prove Mary Louise was the kidnapper. You just want her to be the kidnapper and you don't want to offer a reward."

I was so angry I couldn't say anything. Why was he always taking Lily's side? Was he hiding something? If I didn't know him better I'd swear he was.

"Kevin and Reggie are going to the movies tomorrow night," said Maxine. "I think we should go and spy on them."

"Wait a minute," I complained. "Mary Louise's the one to watch."

"Then *you* watch her," yelled Joey.

"I don't have time to argue anymore," said Maxine, putting her notebook in her backpack. "I have to go home. Give me back my ski mask."

"It's under the bed." I reached into the pile of clothes but couldn't find it. "It's probably in one of Mom's sneakers." I ran into Mom's bedroom, but the sneakers were empty.

"So where is it?" asked Maxine.

"Uh oh. I hate to tell you, but the last I remember is taking the ski mask off in Mary Louise's closet."

"Oh, no!" said Joey.

"How could you?" said Maxine. "This is horrendous."

"I'm sorry. I didn't lose your ski mask on purpose."

"What are you going to do?" Maxine put her hands on her hips. "I told you to wait for me before you searched her room. I said it wasn't a good idea."

"Let's go back to her house."

"There's no way to get in," said Maxine. "They've installed a burglar alarm."

"*I* can get in."

"You said you'd never do that again," said Maxine.

"But I have to get your ski mask."

"Forget that," said Joey. "Finish your article. We'll find Lester without you."

"Wait a minute. I say we should —"

"We don't need you — you keep causing trouble. You write your article. We're going to make a reward flier."

"And we're going to spy on Kevin and Reggie at the movie," said Maxine, as they left. "Let us know if you find out anything on Mary Louise or my ski mask."

"I don't need you either," I said, and slammed the door.

Mom collapsed on the couch when she came home. "You wouldn't believe how awful my day was."

"Oh, yes, I would."

"The store was a mess from yesterday's sale. People ripped open boxes and threw things under counters. Why do I work there? I need another job."

She looked tired and she had more wrinkles around her eyes than usual.

"Do you want me to make you a cup of tea?"

"That would be wonderful, dear."

I wanted to tell her about Lester, but when I brought the tea she said, "I drove on the highway this afternoon. Takes your breath away, there's so many cars. I practiced getting on and off. Got on at Russell and off at the park, turned around and went back six times. Mmmm, this tea is good. I wish I could just sit here all night, but I have to distribute an *Alert* newsletter about the break-in at the O'Briens'."

I froze. "What about the break-in?"

"We have to let all our neighbors know so they can be aware of what happened and take precautions. This is the first crime in our neighborhood in a year. It's terrible. Just terrible." I felt ill. "So I have to get an *Alert* out to everyone in our section and to all the other captains in our group. I wrote the newsletter and typed it during my lunch hour. The copy place said my order would be ready by seven-thirty." She finished her tea. "What were you up to this afternoon?"

"Doing interviews. I'm writing an article on the smartest girls at Saint Anne's."

"That's a good project — and a good goal. Why, I bet if you put your mind to it *you* could be one of the smartest girls at Saint Anne's."

"Sure, Mom." I started for the door.

"Don't run away when I tell you something you don't want to hear."

I was halfway down the hall to my room.

"You're just as smart as Mary Louise."

"Mom, please."

"You'd better listen to me or someday you'll be sorry when you have to get a job like mine and Mary Louise is a famous doctor or lawyer."

I threw my backpack on the floor and kicked it. I'd had enough of Mary Louise and everybody else I knew. What was I going to do about Maxine's ski mask? And what was I going to do about Lester?

· 16 ·

The Spy in the Movie Theater

By the middle of Saturday afternoon, I was tired of being alone. I missed Joey and Maxine. I wanted to join them and spy on Kevin and Reggie. I told Mom, "Maxine and Joey are going to the movies. Can I go, too?"

"What's playing?"

"*The Creature from Zargon.*"

Mom looked surprised.

"It's supposed to be great. Everyone's going. The early show starts at five-thirty."

"Is your article done?"

After I promised to finish the article, clean my room, and write to Grandma, Mom said I could go. She arranged for Ernie to give me a ride home.

Joey and Maxine's reward fliers were in a rack at the theater. They'd done a nice job: the flier had a picture of Lester sitting up and staring straight out. You could even see the kink in his tail. The caption read:

$20 REWARD $20
For return of LESTER
White Laboratory Rat
Kink in tail
No questions asked
Secrecy guaranteed
Call Joey 843-6019
Maxine 843-9469

I disguised myself in the bathroom with glasses and Dad's black punk wig that he wore to his union's Halloween party. I already had on a sweat shirt and hiking boots. I liked the result: I looked like a boy — fourteen, maybe fifteen years old.

I sat in the back so I could see who came in. As usual, the theater smelled and my feet stuck to the floor. The Elmwood was the largest theater in town and hundreds of kids went there on the weekends.

Within a few minutes, Maxine and Joey arrived, laughing and talking. They looked so happy without me, I felt sad. They sat off to the side, about ten rows in front of me. When a family sat in the row behind them, I moved next to the family.

Joey was saying, "It's been fifty hours since Lester was kidnapped. We should have offered a reward right away instead of listening to Maria. She always thinks she knows everything."

"She was trying to help," said Maxine.

"She only wants to find Lester so she can do her magic act."

"C'mon, Joey. She cares about Lester. Because of him she has to write an article."

"That's her own fault. She made up the article. Lester's my rat and she acts like he's still hers — like I might sell him back to her if she wanted. I wouldn't sell Lester to her. I wouldn't sell him to anybody. He's my rat — forever."

I gulped. I'd always hoped he'd sell Lester back to me someday.

"She made me mad when she went to Mary Louise's without me," said Maxine. "She doesn't know as much about detective work as I do."

I slumped in my seat. These were my two best friends talking. And they didn't seem to like me.

When I got up to leave, Maxine said, "Hey! Look who's here!"

I froze, but she was pointing to Mary Louise and Lily. That's when I decided to stay and spy on everybody.

"Maria better do something about my ski mask," said Maxine. "My name's in it. If Mary Louise finds it, she'll blame me for the break-in."

"Do you think Mary Louise kidnapped Lester?"

"No. I think Kevin did."

"You think Kevin does everything. What about Reggie?"

"Or Lily?"

The lights dimmed and the movie started.

"Don't you get on her case like Maria does."

"Shush," said the family in back of them.

In the movie: *A group of creatures left an island far away and swam into the sea. They swam for many days, finally emerging onto a deserted beach. Their tall bodies, covered with iridescent scales, sent shafts of shimmering light into the early morning fog.*

Drums beat softly as the creatures paused to talk, then separated to begin their search for the land's inhabitants.

"Kevin and Reggie are here," said Maxine. "Don't let them see us."

She and Joey slid down in their chairs. They didn't have to worry because Kevin and Reggie were eating popcorn from a huge tub and yelling to friends. They sat in the first row and ignored people telling them to be quiet. When Kevin belched, Reggie broke up as if the belch were the most hilarious thing in the world.

I wrote in my notebook: K gross and R dumb. J and M don't care about me.

One of the creatures tried to talk to a farmer driving a tractor, but the farmer got frightened and drove away. The creature chased the farmer. The farmer panicked and ran over the creature.

While the audience screamed during the chase, Maxine

and Joey moved to the row behind Kevin and Reggie, and I moved to the row behind Mary Louise and Lily.

Lily was showing Mary Louise the flier. "What . . . rat . . . how?"

Because of the movie, I couldn't hear them. Praying I wouldn't be recognized, I moved to an empty seat in front of Lily and scrunched down.

"That kid's hair is bizarre," said Mary Louise about my wig. I could hear perfectly now. "Strange that Maria's name isn't on this flier."

"Lester isn't her rat anymore," said Lily.

"Doesn't matter. You know Maria. Everybody's business is her business. I wonder if the people who broke into my house had something to do with the kidnapping. Oh, gross, they're shooting a creature with fire — I can't look."

"I'm not going to look either," said Lily. "Maybe we should help find Lester. Joey was really worried."

"No way," shouted Mary Louise.

"Be quiet," said people around us.

Covered with flames, the leader of the creatures dove off the cliff into the bay. A group of jeering townspeople hovered at the cliff's edge, hoping the creature was dead, but he wasn't. He swam to safety in the rocks by the shore.

Mary Louise whispered, "Marie better do a good write-up on me in her article or she'll be sorry. Sister Margaret's not going to put up with any more of her fooling around."

"Why did you tell Sister Margaret on her?" whispered Lily.

The creature watched a car being forced off the road above the cliff. The car spun and bounced off the rocks on its long drop to the bay.

"Her magic act's too good. I was afraid Sister Margaret might pick her over us, so I tried to get her disqualified."

"Sister Margaret said she'd pick three acts from our class."

"I heard her tell Sister Agnes that she liked the singing altar boys and Najuma's flute playing. We need all the help we can get to beat Maria."

"You didn't make her ruin the teddy bear, did you?"

"No, we were lucky."

"But you wouldn't do anything . . . I mean you —"

The creature in the bay swam to the car and rescued a woman. He carried her gently onto the beach. Meanwhile, in a supermarket parking lot, a group of men on motorcycles closed in on the last two creatures from the sea.

"Do you want to go to Disneyland with the talent show winners or do you want to stay here helping Maria?"

Machine-gun fire from the movie obliterated Lily's response.

When the gunfire stopped, Mary Louise was saying, "We'll get to wear lipstick and eye make-up, too."

While they talked about their costumes for the show, I decided to move to the empty seat next to Reggie. Kevin was sitting on Reggie's right and behind Reggie were Joey and Maxine.

I kept my head down and rushed into the seat.

"Watch it, dude, you almost stepped on my foot," said Reggie.

"What happened to your hair?" sneered Kevin. "Looks like my mom cut it."

I pretended I had found a reward flier under my chair. "This yours?" I asked Reggie in my deepest voice.

"Yeah." He grabbed it and nudged Kevin. "Here's the flier I told you about."

Kevin whistled as he read it.

"Who do you think did it?" asked Reggie.

"You," said Kevin. "Ha, ha."

Reggie punched Kevin's arm. "Don't be funny."

"Be quiet. Shut up," said people around us.

"You're the type."

"Hey, look," said Reggie. "I used to think I could sell Lester to a lab and make money, but my uncle who works in a lab said they only buy rats from breeders. So—"

"Don't get excited," said Kevin. "Have some popcorn."

But Reggie was excited. "I know how we can get the reward money."

I held my breath.

"My uncle can get a rat that looks like Lester. We'll give the rat to Joey and get the reward."

"Never work," said Kevin, stuffing popcorn into his mouth and smearing butter across his chin. "Lester can do tricks. But I'd like to get my hands on a pile of money."

"We'll teach another rat those tricks."

"Give it up," said Kevin, grabbing the flier. "Maria's name isn't on here — wonder what that means."

"She's probably grounded. You should have seen what she did to a teddy bear yesterday. Sick city. I think Sister Agnes blasted her."

"I hope so. Maria thinks she knows everything."

How come everyone thought I thought I knew everything?

The creature took the woman to her home. He watched the deaths of his friends on television. He saw the army and navy launch massive efforts to find him.

"Twenty dollars buys a lot of video games."

"Get off my back with your crazy ideas," said Kevin. Reggie kept trying to convince Kevin to trick Joey. I wrote in my notebook: Reggie couldn't have Lester — if he did, he'd turn Lester in himself for the money.

"Maybe Maria took the rat," said Kevin. "Maybe she got tired of Joey and my dumb sister."

"Yeah," said Reggie. "Then she'd be the Amazing Valvano all by herself and not have to include her friends."

Even Reggie and Kevin thought I was a creep. Did anyone like me?

The huge creature looked longingly at the town. He wanted to stay and be part of it, but everyone hated him so he had to go. He only wanted to be friends. Why didn't they understand?

When the creature returned to the sea to swim back to his island, I got up and left, wiping tears from my eyes.

I stumbled through the lobby as fast as I could. Out on the street people stared at me. As I pulled the wig off I tripped and my hand banged my nose, making it bleed. I was asking a man for a tissue when I heard: "Maria Valvano, you're not begging, are you?"

It was Mrs. Bossi in a red dress with white polka dots. I wiped my nose on my sleeve and shoved the wig into my pocket, but I could feel a trickle of warm liquid crossing my upper lip.

"Your nose is bleeding!" She put her hand on my shoulder and whispered, "I saw a program on drug abuse — you're not having an OD, are you?"

The polka dots weren't evenly spread out on her dress. They were bunched up in places and it made me dizzy to look at them.

The line for the seven-thirty show was forming. I wanted to leave before I saw anyone I knew, but my right foot had fallen asleep. I tried a step. My ankle wobbled, then gave out, pitching me forward onto the biggest bunch of polka dots that targeted Mrs. Bossi's stomach.

"Go home, Maria," she said, her voice muffled by my hair. "You don't want to break your mother's heart, do you?"

People were coming out of the movie. I put the wig back on so no one would recognize me.

"Eaahh! That's not your rat, is it?"

"No," I almost screamed. But I had to act as if everything were okay — otherwise I knew she'd tell Mom. "It's just a wig, Mrs. Bossi, a disguise. I'm helping Maxine with her detective work. Are you going to the movie?"

Mrs. Bossi gave me a piercing look that seemed to say, "What's going on here?"

I kept talking. "The movie's quite good. I know you'll love it. I can't wait to get home and tell Mom. My ride should be here any —"

"Hey, Maria. Over here. Jeez, what a crowd." Ernie's truck had just pulled up to the corner.

I said a prayer of thanks and staggered over to him, moaning, "This is the worst day of my life." I got into the car and told him the whole story — everything — ending with "Reggie and Lily are innocent."

"Two suspects knocked out? Say now, that's not bad for two days' work, even if the detectives are no longer speaking to each other. But promise me one thing: no more going into other people's houses. Promise?"

"I *had* to do it — to save Lester."

"Hold on a minute. You didn't *have* to do it. You don't have to do everything you think of. Listen, Maria, you go overboard on things sometimes. And this time you broke the law."

"I didn't mean to."

"Not everyone is going to believe you."

That got me. "What if someone finds out I was the one who broke into Mary Louise's? Will I go to jail?"

"You'd have to ask your mom."

"No way. Never."

"Hey. You *have* to tell your mom."

"I have to? Even if I promise not to go back to Mary Louise's?"

"Jeez, I'm glad to hear that. But yes, you have to tell your mom. Maybe not today but sometime soon — like before the end of next week."

"I'll try. But I've got another question: what should I do about Maxine's ski mask?"

"Don't do anything. Wait and see. Maybe you lost it on the way home. C'mon, Maria. Go with the flow."

· 17 ·

The Fortune in
the Fortune Cookie

Saturday night I lay in bed wishing I *could* go with the flow. I'd tried but I couldn't. And to make matters worse, I didn't know why everyone said I thought I knew everything. So I told people what to do. Was that so bad? I guess it was or Joey and Maxine wouldn't be mad at me.

I turned over on my side and promised to make a new start the next day. The trouble was that each start led to disaster. If I apologized to Maxine and told Mary Louise I was the one who left the ski mask in her closet, then she'd tell her mom and her mom would tell the police. If I told my mom what I had done, then since she was the neighborhood crime-watch captain, she'd have to tell the police, too. No matter how I looked at it, I was going to end up in jail.

If Mary Louise had Lester then I was in the clear. I think. But I had to find Lester to prove that. Where could Mary Louise be hiding him?

Every time I closed my eyes I saw Lester — twitching his nose, cuddling between my feet, running across my room. I fell asleep and dreamed I was searching for him. I had run for miles through a strange city calling Lester when suddenly he was ahead of me. But no matter how fast I ran I never got close enough to catch him.

Along the side streets were little jail houses with my name on them and policemen reaching out at me. Occasionally, one would grab my arm or my shoulder and I'd moan and struggle to get away.

Lester ran into a huge theater and I followed. All the suspects were running down the aisles to the stage and each suspect had a Lester. Lily had Lester peeking out of her bag. Mary Louise had Lester in Maxine's ski mask and she was twirling it as she ran. Kevin had Lester in the pocket of his backpack. Lester was squeaking at me to help.

I didn't know which suspect to run after. Reggie was already on the stage juggling four Lesters. And riding around him on a bike was a masked person with Lester sitting on his shoulder throwing cheese at me. I ran after the masked person, yelling, "Who are you? Who are you?"

"Maria, wake up. It's me — Mom. You're having a bad dream." Mom was shaking my shoulder. "You're okay. I'm here. Don't worry." She hugged me and rubbed my back.

"I had a terrible dream about Lester."

"Do you want to tell me about it?"

"Later." I didn't know how to explain Maxine's ski mask and the jail houses.

"Whatever you want. Why don't you get up now and have breakfast?"

All Sunday morning I tried to act as though everything was okay, but it wasn't easy because I was so worried about Lester. Then Mrs. Bossi stopped by to drive us to church and I was afraid she was going to tell Mom about running into me in front of the theater. She didn't say anything, but she gave me a few piercing looks.

At Mass I sat between Mom and Mrs. Bossi. Mrs. Bossi's dress had black and white stripes. The stripes on the top were horizontal but the stripes in the skirt were vertical. The dress reminded me of zebras and made me wish I could move to Africa and begin my life over.

I was thinking what a great hunter I'd be when Father Columbo waved a piece of paper at us and announced that his sermon was going to be on pride, the deadliest of sins. "The Lord works in mysterious ways. When he knew I was going to talk about pride, he put this fortune in my fortune cookie: 'The showoff will be shown up at the showdown.'

"Now, I want all of you to think about what that means in your lives. Think of all the times you show off

— when you brag about the special things you can do or when you tell people that *you* know what they should do. Showoffs think they know more than anyone else."

Mrs. Bossi elbowed me and gave me another piercing look. Mom was staring at the altar.

Father Columbo concluded, "I want you to give that up and God wants you to give that up because in the big showdown, that showdown of showdowns at the end of the world, God will sit in judgment and you will be shown up. You could end up in hell forever, because of pride."

"I knew it," said Mrs. Bossi.

I thought about the sermon. I guess I was a showoff sometimes, but I was trying to find Lester. And so what if he wasn't my rat anymore? I still cared about him — a lot. And not just because of the magic show either. Lester needed my help. Sister Margaret said to get my priorities straight and Lester was my first priority. I *had* to find him no matter who liked me or not.

On the way out, Mrs. Bossi whispered, "I hope you got the message."

"I did," I assured her. "I really did."

At home Mom read my article. "This is good, Maria. Just a few spelling mistakes. I'm telling you, you could be one of the smartest girls in your class."

"Mom, forget it."

"Don't be rude. I'm going to the supermarket with Mrs. Bossi. I'll be back in an hour. If you clean the living room, I'll take you to the park and buy you an ice cream."

I had to tell Mom about Lester soon. Maybe at the park.

I fixed my article, then vacuumed the living room. When Dad was home he did pushups every morning in the living room, leaving handprints in the rug. And when I came home from school I'd see the handprints and feel safe even though the house was empty. But now there weren't any handprints, the house was empty, and worst of all, I didn't feel safe. Any minute I could be sent to jail.

"What's the matter?" asked Mom when she returned. "You look as if you've lost your best friend. Come to think of it, I haven't seen Maxine in ages. What's going on?"

"I, well . . ." I didn't know where to begin.

"Did you have a fight or something?"

"Sort of."

"I know you, Maria. You can be pretty bossy about things."

Even my own mom felt that way.

She followed me down the hall. "Why don't you call Maxine and say you're sorry? It doesn't hurt to be the first one to apologize."

That's when I gave Mom a reward flier and said, "Lester's been kidnapped."

"Oh, no. Not another crime in our neighborhood."

"Yes, and he was kidnapped from our house last Thursday."

"The day of the inventory sale?"

"Yes. I came home and the downstairs door was open and the spare key was in our lock." Mom was gasping so much I wondered if I should get her a glass of water.

"Don't stop. Go on with the story," she said, gasping even more.

"Well, I came inside and while I was looking to see if anything had been stolen, the kidnapper ran outside with Lester and a bunch of my magic act props. I never even saw the kidnapper because by the time I got to the street no one was there. Even Bud hadn't noticed anyone."

"Oh! This is terrible. My poor baby. Anything could have happened. Thank heavens the kidnapper only took the rat. Oh! I have to call Mrs. Bossi right away. We have to have another crime-watch meeting. Why didn't you tell me this sooner?"

"Because . . . I thought the kidnapper was Mary Louise and I — I —"

"Don't be ridiculous, Maria. A smart girl like Mary Louise would never take someone else's rat. Oh! Please make me a cup of tea."

"But, Mom — I have to ask you something." Mom had already crossed the room and picked up the phone. "Is it really a crime to use someone else's spare key to get into that person's house?"

"Of course. It's illegal to go into someone else's home." Mom began dialing.

"Even if you think that person stole something of yours?"

"Yes, yes, yes. Now go make me a cup of tea. Hello, Ada? We have to have a meeting tonight and send out another *Alert*. I just found out about another break-in . . . yes, it *is* terrible . . . last week . . . my house . . . she's all right . . . yes, right away . . . at the church auditorium."

I went to make Mom's tea while she called other coordinators. I felt doomed. I wanted to tell Mom about Mary Louise but I was afraid she'd bring me to the meeting and they'd all carry me to jail.

When I brought Mom her tea she was writing the agenda for the meeting.

"Thanks, dear. No wonder you were having nightmares. We'll have to talk about this a lot more. Wait till your father hears. I'd send him a telegram — but he'd only worry." Mom took a huge drink of tea. "I'm going to the crime-watch meeting. You do your homework. Don't let anyone in and call if anything bothers you. I hate to leave you alone but I'll be home in a couple of hours." She gave me a hug and left, saying, "I'll bring home a pizza for dinner."

I walked through our apartment, wondering how much longer I'd be able to live there. I turned on the television, but everything was absolutely boring. There was only one thing to do — study for tomorrow's history test. I could ace it and show those smart girls that I could be just as smart as them. I liked that idea. Besides, if I got a good grade on the test, Mom might not disown me when she found out the truth about the break-in.

· 18 ·

The Urgent, Crucial Message

Monday morning I waved to Maxine on her way to school, but she didn't wait for me. At the light she looked back, held my gaze for a moment, then walked on without me.

I handed in the article on the smartest girls and suffered through the history test. I had to admit the test was easier because I'd studied for it.

During school I caught Maxine looking at me a few times. Each time I smiled, but she looked away. Joey didn't look at me at all. He stared at Lily. Why did I think he was a good friend? So he was nice to animals and liked Lester. What did that prove? Nothing.

At recess I tried to talk to Maxine and Joey. "Hey, you guys did a nice job on the reward flier."

"Oh, hi, Maria," said Joey. "Thanks. We tried to make it as good as possible."

"Any new evidence?" asked Maxine.

"Well, not exactly. You, uh, were right about going back to Mary Louise's. So I didn't go."

"Good," said Maxine. "I was worried."

I think she smiled a little, but I wasn't sure. She and Joey weren't too friendly.

"Any word on Lester?" I asked.

"No, and it's been ninety-one hours since Lester was kidnapped. I just hope he's alive."

"Me, too." I'd hoped *someone* would answer the reward flier. "I told my mother about Lester's kidnapping. She got pretty upset and called a crime-watch meeting. They even put out another *Alert*."

"I saw it," said Joey. "There's a copy of the reward flier in it."

"What's happening with Mary Louise and my ski mask?" asked Maxine, opening her notebook.

"Nothing, and I'm *really* sorry. But don't worry—if Mary Louise finds your ski mask I'll confess."

"Yeah. Well, thanks." Maxine started to walk away. "See you around."

"What about the magic show?" I asked.

"I'll let you know tomorrow," said Maxine.

"Yeah. Me, too," said Joey.

I felt so badly I hid in the bathroom until recess was over. And at lunchtime, I ate alone outside, looking through a cafeteria window, watching Joey and Maxine laugh together. Again the idea came to me: what if Joey had kidnapped Lester? It seemed ridiculous: Joey owned Lester, Joey was my friend.

After school Joey and Lily left together. He didn't seem to be suffering with worry over Lester. He looked happy — too happy. The more I thought about it, the more I wondered if Joey was the kidnapper.

He didn't want Lester to be in the magic show. He left school before me the day of the kidnapping. He knew where my key was. He knew what the magic show props were. *He knew everything.*

I didn't want to believe Joey had kidnapped Lester. I wanted Mary Louise to be the kidnapper — I didn't like *her*. But I had to face reality. Besides, no one had been to Joey's house since the kidnapping. He could be hiding Lester there. And I bet he loved telling Lily the tragic story of his pet's kidnapping.

I *had* to talk to Maxine about this.

At the frozen yogurt shop on Washington Street, Joey bought Lily a cup of fresh peach dipped in chocolate and got himself a cone with two scoops of nutty mint banana.

When they left the shop a flier fell out of Joey's pocket. I waited till they turned the corner, then picked it up and read:

* * HELP WANTED * *
BIRTHDAY MAGIC, INC., NEEDS
CLOWNS, DANCERS, SINGERS & MAGICIANS
WE WANT ADULTS, CHILDREN & ANIMALS
TO PERFORM AT LOCAL PARTIES
HIRING *NOW* — GOOD PAY

Now this was very interesting. It could mean a lot of things. And one of the things might be that Joey had kidnapped Lester so that he could work on his own magic act. Then Joey could get a job with this place and make big money.

The flier could mean a lot of other things. But I didn't want to take any chances. So I ran home and called Maxine. Her line was busy. I was still trying when Mom came home.

"Today we reviewed everything. Only one more lesson to go till my driver's test. Mr. Anson thinks I'll do fine. You've got to question me on the whole book tonight."

I promised to help Mom and called Maxine again. This time her parents' answering machine was on. I wished I'd listened to her and made up a secret code. I left the message: *Call Maria. Urgent. Crucial.*

At eight-thirty Maxine called back.

"I've wanted to talk to you so much," I said.

"What's your urgent, crucial message?" she asked.

"It's about me . . . I, uh, I want to apologize for losing

your hat and" — my voice dropped to a whisper — "for acting like I think I know everything."

"Oh, Maria," said Maxine.

"I guess sometimes I can't help being bossy. But I'm going to try not to be."

I could hear her sigh. Then I felt so embarrassed that before she could say anything I changed the subject and said, "I have to tell you something else. You're not going to believe me. In fact, I don't think I can even tell you."

"Maria, tell me. I can't stand it."

"I think Joey might be the kidnapper."

There was a great silence until she said, "Is this a joke?"

"No, I'm super serious."

"I can't believe you're telling me this."

I told her everything.

"Joey could have found the flier," she said. "Maybe he was going to show it to us. There's a hundred explanations for it. Besides, what about Mary Louise?"

"Well, I don't have any more information on her and believe me, I'd love to find some. But right now I think we have to check out Joey."

"Maria, I hate to say this but you're sounding like you think you know everything again. I can't believe Joey's guilty. I've been getting along fine with him. Remember how you used to wish I'd be friends with Joey?"

"Yeah, I remember." After all the worry over them,

who would have thought things would turn out this way? "We have to face the facts."

"I don't know. You're jumping to a big conclusion. What if you're making a mistake?"

"I don't have an answer to that question."

Maxine was quiet and I was afraid she was thinking I was making a mistake, but then she said, "However, if you're right, this is incredible. I'll tell you one thing — my guide says the culprit is often the one you least suspect."

I could just picture Maxine in her armchair with her Sherlock Holmes hat on.

"We have to proceed cautiously," she said. "What do you want to do?"

"Three things: watch him very carefully to see if he slips up, get him to come to a strategy meeting about Lester and the magic act tomorrow, and surprise him at his house to see if Lester or any of the props are there."

"Okay, partner," she said.

That was the nicest thing I'd heard in days.

· 19 ·

A Trail of Gushing Water

The next morning Maxine and I surprised Joey at his house before school.

"C'mon in," he said. "But I don't think you know what you're getting into."

"I've been here before, Joey," said Maxine.

"I've been busy — with the reward flier and searching for Lester," he explained as we walked down the hall to his room. "I haven't had much time to straighten up."

"You can say that again," I said.

"Maria!" Maxine shot me a look. I had promised to let her be in charge of the investigation.

Maxine went into Joey's room first. I heard her gasp. My first thought was "She's found Lester," but when I walked into the room I gasped, too. It was the biggest mess I'd ever seen in my entire life.

Every surface in his room was covered — with dirty clothes, crumpled papers, cruddy dishes, open books.

Clothes were leaping out of drawers and falling off shelves. There was even a glass with fungus in it and a plate with something on it that made me gag.

"Joey? What? How?" I asked. Less than two weeks ago this room was normal.

Joey shrugged. "How can I clean up when Lester's held captive somewhere?"

I could barely walk — ankle-deep piles of dirty clothes mired the floor. Oozing over the piles were: baseball mitt and hat, blankets, baseball cards, comic books. I couldn't see the top of his desk and I couldn't even guess how many layers were there.

Still, I didn't give up hope. I worked my way to his closet, slipping on three baseball cards and the cover of a comic book. But I didn't find anything — not Lester, his cage, or any of the stolen props — only jackets, pants, games, and another pile of dirty clothes.

"I told you you were way off base," whispered Maxine.

"This doesn't prove he doesn't have Lester," I whispered back. "He's got other places in the house, he's —"

"What are you two up to?" asked Joey.

"Nothing." I turned away.

"You can say that again," said Maxine, writing *Nothing* in her notebook.

"We'd better go or we'll be late for school. And I hate to say this but it's now one hundred and thirteen hours since Lester was kidnapped."

"What did you do with Lester's things?" I asked. "The ones you used to keep on the shelf by the window?"

"They're in the spare room. I'm going to have an animal collection in there."

"Can we see?"

"Sure."

I practically ran behind Joey to the spare room, but again nothing — except for the things of Lester's that Joey had bought.

Maxine put her hand on my shoulder. "Let's go."

We told Joey everything that had happened on the way to school. He agreed to come to a strategy meeting but made it clear he wasn't too interested in the magic show.

"We don't have a chance to win without Lester," he said.

"I think we should try. I'm sure I can come up with something."

"I don't know," he said. "You know where your last idea got us."

"Yeah," said Maxine. "Into a mess."

I could see they were never going to let me forget.

When we got to school Sister Margaret called me to her desk.

"So, Miss Pulitzer Prize, your article's not bad. You did a good job. I'm going to print it in the newspaper. I especially liked your *Guide to a Superior Mind*. And I'm glad to see you've begun to use yours."

"I . . ." I was confused.

"Looks as though you followed your own advice. You got an A on the history test. Congratulations."

It felt weird having Sister Margaret say something nice to me. I practically bounced to my seat. But before I got there she dealt me a body blow.

"By the way, Maria, don't forget that tomorrow's the audition. I hope you've got your act to work."

What was I going to do? Joey and Maxine needed something big to convince them to do the act. I couldn't do it alone. All during math I thought about Lester and his rabbit costume. Finally, I got an inspiration. I was sure it would work.

I sent Maxine a note:

I'VE GOT A GREAT IDEA. MEET ME AT RECESS.

Unfortunately, Sister Margaret intercepted it.

"Really, Maria. You never learn, do you? I'll see you in detention today."

She kept me in during recess and I watched Maxine walk away.

At lunch time I was right behind Maxine in the hall but Sister Agnes stopped me. "Congratulations, Maria. Your article is well written and informative. I knew you

could do it. I can't wait to see your magic act at the
audition tomorrow. I'll be praying for you."

By the time I caught up with Maxine she and Joey
had decided we'd meet after dinner to talk about my idea.

After school Sister Margaret kept me only ten minutes
but lectured me every second. "I'm letting you go early,
Maria, because I know you'll want to work on your act."

Boy, was she right on target.

I got my stuff and left school as fast as I could. I figured if I ran I could catch up to Maxine and Joey. We
needed lots of time to work on my idea.

As I ran out the school gate I noticed water gushing
down the street. Not a simple stream of water but a huge,
foot-splashing, torrent of water. A book bag floated by,
then a lunch box.

Drains overflowed, flooding the streets. In the next
block I saw a kindergarten kid being rescued. In the
block after that John and Jesse from my class were wad-
ing in water above their knees.

"You'd better get out of there," I yelled.

Horns blared and sirens shrieked. It seemed that all the
kids in town were running toward Washington Street.
The traffic was blocked even on the side streets. Kevin
and his friends were filling balloons with water and
throwing them at cars.

I ran behind a bush so they wouldn't spot me.

At the corner I saw Ernie's truck.

"Hey, Maria," he yelled. "What a mess! You got a good alibi?"

"I didn't do it," I yelled back and kept running. I couldn't see Maxine anywhere.

When I turned onto Washington Street, a ton of water was squirting up into the air — just like pictures of Old Faithful. It went higher than the bank building and that was five stories high. It was the most water I'd ever seen in my life.

"The car plowed right into that hydrant," said a man in front of me.

Two firemen were dragging the hydrant along the street. Behind them on the sidewalk, with a dented grill, was the car. In the crowd around it were kids from my class — Joey and Lily, Najuma and Sylvie, Wayne and Reggie, and Maxine, writing in her notebook.

I pushed through the crowd to talk to her but Sister Margaret jogged between us, shouting, "What's going on here?"

"That car ran right up onto the sidewalk," said a woman in a red coat.

The crowd parted and I saw the sign PARADISE DRIVER EDUCATION — Mom's driving school. And there was Mom talking to two policemen. A man next to her handed them papers from his briefcase. I bet he was her instructor, Mr. Anson.

Mary Louise ran up to Lily and Najuma and whispered loudly, "That's Maria's mother." The whispering spread out in waves around me — getting louder as it passed from one person to another — until it was a chant: *Maria's mother, Maria's mother.*

I felt so hot I thought my clothes would burn off. Kids looked at me, then turned away. Others stared with their mouths open.

I wished I could disappear. How could Mom do this to me?

But what if she'd been hurt? I ran to her, yelling, "Mom, Mom, are you okay?"

"Of course, dear." She hugged me as I buried myself in her arms.

"How are we going to pay for the car?"

"The school has insurance."

"And the hydrant?"

"Jeez, they've got more hydrants where that one came from."

"Ernie!" said Mom. "Am I glad to see you."

"You ladies need a ride home?"

"Do we ever!" Mom told Mr. Anson she'd see him later and we ran to Ernie's truck.

"I'm so embarrassed," said Mom. Then she looked at Ernie and laughed. He laughed, too.

"How can you laugh?" I asked. "I'm embarrassed, too."

Mom poked me while Ernie opened the truck door.

"What are *you* embarrassed about? I'm the one who was driving."

"Mom, everybody I know was there."

"Hey," said Ernie as he drove off. "No one noticed my hair."

"I like the cut," said Mom. "Makes you look younger."

"I like the smell," I said, wondering what it reminded me of. "But where's the gray?"

"C'mon, Maria, give me a break."

· 20 ·

The Truth about the Break-in

When the doorbell rang I didn't want to answer it. "What if it's the police?"

"Go ahead, Maria," said Mom. "We have to face the music sometime."

I opened the door expecting the worst.

I got worse than the worst: I got Mary Louise.

"Go away," I said and closed the door.

"Oh, no, you don't," she said.

"Oh, yes, I do," I shouted.

She banged on the door. "You better let me in or you'll never see Maxine again."

I yanked open the door and Mary Louise waved Maxine's ski mask in my face. "Recognize this?"

I felt sick. "C'mon in. We'll talk in my room."

We walked past Mom on the phone. She looked surprised to see Mary Louise.

"Okay," I said, when we were in my bedroom. "What do you want?"

"A lot," she said. "The only time this ski mask could have gotten into my closet was during the break-in. And if I tell, Maxine will be in the biggest trouble of her life. So if you don't want that to happen, you'd better do as I say."

"Just tell me what you want, Mary Louise."

"I want you to drop out of the show."

"You've got to be kidding."

"I *never* kid." She looked in my mirror and smoothed her disgustingly perfect blond hair, smiled at herself, and turned to me. "*Never.*"

"That's not fair. You're cheating. You know my act is good."

"But *I* want to win, so you better do as I say."

"But —"

"I bet anything you were involved in the break-in, Maria. Unfortunately, I can't prove that. However, if I have to, I'll tell that Maxine was." She smiled at herself in the mirror and smoothed her hair one more time. "Don't get up. I know how to get out."

She didn't have to worry about my getting up. I was too stunned to move.

A little later Mom came into my room. "Wasn't that nice of Mary Louise to drop by. See — not everyone thinks it's terrible that your mother knocked over a hydrant."

*   *   *

When the doorbell rang again I yelled, "I'm not answering it."

Mom yelled back, "You have to. I'm on the phone with Mr. Anson."

With a heavy heart I buzzed the front door, closed my eyes, and opened the door.

"Want some company?" asked Maxine. "Whenever my mom does something embarrassing I want to hide."

"Am I glad to see you," I said, hugging her. I didn't know how to begin to tell her.

"At least your mom doesn't make you look funny," she said. "Remember when my mom gave me a permanent and my hair came out too tight? I had to wear a scarf to school."

I didn't laugh.

"What's the matter? You don't look so good."

"Let's go into my bedroom. I have something serious to tell you." I closed the door. "Mary Louise was here. She found your ski mask and she wants us to drop out of the show or she's going to say that you did the break-in."

Maxine sat down slowly. "Incredible."

"Don't worry," I said. "We'll drop out of the show. If she still tries to tell anyone, I'll confess. I'll say I was the only one. I'll —"

"Wait," said Maxine. "I just have to think about this for a minute."

We took our usual places when we thought in my room. Maxine sat in the chair at my desk. I sat on my bed.

Maxine looked through her notebook, then said, "Funny. I was going to try to convince you that I'm sure the kidnapper is Kevin." She wrote on the suspect chart: WHERE IS HE EVERY AFTERNOON? "He works at the shop and goes to the video parlor, but that doesn't account for all the time he's away from home. I know he's up to something."

"Maxine, our big problem is Mary Louise."

"I know, I know. My question is: what if she's doing this as a way to throw us off her track? I mean, your first thought would not be that she has Lester."

"Absolutely not," I said. "Why would she come over here if she had Lester?"

"To make sure we're not in the show. See? What if she kidnapped Lester to try to end our act? But that didn't stop us. So she had to do something else and unfortunately, you played into her hands by leaving my ski mask in her closet."

"This is too much for me." I put my head down on my bed. "You are some detective, Maxine. But even if she took Lester she still has your ski mask. What are we going to do about that?"

"Don't forget we know that she didn't go right to the dance studio the day of the kidnapping. I don't think she wants certain people to know she did that."

"Boy, would I love to tell that to Sister Margaret."

"We'll decide what to do about Mary Louise when Joey comes tonight." Maxine pointed to the suspect chart. "Right now, time for a review." She tapped Kevin's picture. "Kevin is still a prime suspect for me. What about you?"

"No. I wouldn't put it past him but I think it's Mary Louise or Joey."

"Mary Louise is prime for me, too. I'd love to convict her."

"Now you're talking." I walked over and joined Maxine at my desk.

"Reggie's out."

"Yeah," I said. "I'm glad. I felt sorry for him when Sister Margaret turned his act down."

"Not me. Lily's out, too. Right?"

"Right." I hated to admit that. "Let's not leave out Joey."

"Maria, I still think you're making a mistake about him."

"Wait and see what he says tonight."

At dinner Mom told us she could still take her driver's test. "Mr. Anson said I should get right back in the car: Like getting right back on a horse. So we're going for a short drive tonight."

Maxine and I exchanged glances.

"You girls have homework to do?"

"It's done," I said. "Joey's coming over to work on our act."

"That's fine. I don't like leaving you alone lately. Not with all the break-ins we've been having. Thank goodness the neighborhood's been quiet the last few days."

Maxine and I exchanged glances again. I knew we were both wondering what Mom would say if she knew I did one of the break-ins.

"Some team," said Joey when he arrived. "It's been one hundred and twenty-four hours since Lester was kidnapped and we haven't saved him yet." He looked discouraged but not as much as he did after I told him about Mary Louise.

"Now we have to drop out of the audition," he said.

"Maybe not," said Maxine.

"Yeah," I said. "Thanks to Lily we have info on Mary Louise."

"I don't know," said Joey.

"Are we going to let her tell us what to do?" I asked.

"Yes," said Joey. "Look, I'll confess. Then you two can do the show."

"Oh, no, you don't. If anyone's going to confess, it will be me." Was I really saying that? "I'll take *all* the blame. I'll say I went there alone."

"Good idea," said Maxine.

"Huh?" I said. "I was hoping you'd say, 'No, no, don't do that.'"

"I think you have to confess," said Maxine. "That's the only way to stop Mary Louise. Then it doesn't matter what she says or does."

"Yeah," said Joey, looking a lot less discouraged.

I looked from Maxine to Joey wondering if they were joking, but they weren't. I had to face reality. I had to confess.

"Okay. I'll confess. I'll tell Mom tonight. But then you two have to do the act. I have a great idea: we'll use a fake rabbit. We can make one out of a costume like Lester's. I have more fake fur and Mom's other shoulder pad."

"Sister Margaret wants a *real* rabbit," countered Joey.

"There's no way we can get a real rabbit," I shouted.

"Hey, wait, guys," said Maxine. "Why not use a fake rabbit? Everyone's expecting us to mess up in the audition. If we do the saw trick and it works, I bet no one will notice we don't have a real rabbit."

"And if we get off the stage fast," I said, "Sister Margaret will be too busy with the next act to check. Let's do it."

"You're both crazy," said Joey. "If Sister Margaret finds out she'll give us a huge detention. Why don't we do the act without the saw trick?"

"Because it's our best trick," I shouted. "We need it if we're going to win the trip to Disneyland. How come you're so eager to quit? Are you hiding something?"

Joey's eyes wavered. "This is ridiculous. We're bound to get caught. How can you want to do the act with Lester kidnapped?"

"I worry about Lester, too. All the time. But I still want to do the act. Sister Margaret expects us to do it. And so do other people. I'm going to do the act and I think you should, too — especially since I'm confessing."

"Okay," said Joey. "Count me in. But don't complain when Sister Margaret crucifies us."

While I cut fake fur pieces, Maxine sewed them together, and Joey stuffed them with pieces of Mom's old pantyhose.

I took a break to call Ernie and reported: "He'll bring the box at four-thirty tomorrow when he makes his late afternoon delivery to Bud's. He'll even give us a ride to the auditorium. He'd like to watch our act if it's okay with everyone."

"Fine with me," said Maxine, adjusting the ears.

"It's about time for you kids to call it a day," said Mom. "You have school tomorrow."

"Ten more minutes," I begged. "How'd you make out?"

"Great. That was a good idea to drive right away."

"When are you going to get your license?" asked Joey.

"Tomorrow after work — if I don't run into any more hydrants."

"Mom, please."

"That's when we'll be doing our act at the audition," said Maxine.

"I'll come there after my test and let you know what happened. I hope to get there in time to see your act."

Maxine held up the rabbit. "How's he look?"

"Like a rabbit who's had a hard life," said Mom.

"At least he looks like a rabbit," I said. "What more do we want?"

"Lester," said Joey with a sad look in his eyes.

While Mom was tucking me into bed I asked, "What if someone you knew broke into someone's house?"

"Well, that person was committing a crime. You'd have to report them."

"To the police?" I shivered. Maybe I wouldn't confess.

"That depends on a lot of things — like how old the person is, and whether they stole anything. Things like that."

"What if the person didn't steal anything but was just looking for something of hers?"

"It's still a crime to go into someone else's house. Now, Maria, if one of your friends did something wrong, you'd better tell me. That friend may need help to keep from becoming a criminal."

"Mom, she's not a criminal. She — she's me!"

"You!"

"Yes. I broke into Mary Louise's. I had to. Lester's life depended on it. I was sure she had him. So I used her spare key and —"

"Oh, no! How could you? How *could* you? You know better than to do a thing like that. My own daughter, and I'm captain of our neighborhood crime-watch."

"I *had* to."

"Maria, you didn't *have* to. You just don't know when to stop. You made a big mistake, young lady, and you're going to be sorry."

"Am I going to jail?"

"No, but you're not going anyplace else either. Expect to be grounded for a long time."

"What about the audition?"

"I'll let you know in the morning."

Mom stamped out of my room. I fell asleep listening to her talk to Mrs. Bossi on the phone. "Ada, you won't believe this but . . . yes, my own daughter . . . I know . . . I agree. How *could* she?"

· 21 ·

The Clue in the Cat Carrier

In the morning Mom said, "You can go to the audition. But except for that, consider yourself grounded indefinitely. I've called a neighborhood crime-watch meeting for tonight. We'll decide what your punishment should be then."

"At least you're not going to jail," said Maxine as we walked to school. "I couldn't visit you there."

Joey caught up to us at the corner. "I confessed last night, too," he yelled. "Want to hear the song I made up about it?"

"No," Maxine and I said at the same time.

"This is serious," I said.

"I know, I know," said Joey, dancing beside us. "But I couldn't let you take all the blame. My parents said it was brave of me to confess but I'm still going to be punished. They talked to your mom, Maria, and they're going to the crime-watch meeting tonight."

"Who isn't?" I asked.

We practiced our act before school, at recess, and during lunch. After school we went through it one more time and then split up to get into our costumes for the audition.

I told Maxine, "I'll change, then come over to your house so we can put on our make-up together."

"When are you going to tell Mary Louise she's still got competition?"

"On my way to your house."

"You sure you don't want to call her on the phone?"

"No. I want to tell her in person."

I rang Mary Louise's bell in less than fifteen minutes.

"What do you want?" she asked through lips so red with lipstick she looked as if she were bleeding from the mouth.

"Forget about Disneyland."

"What are you talking about?" She squinted at me through a green outlined eye. The other eye was smudged with purple.

"I confessed to doing the break-in."

"So what?" She smoothed her hot pink leotard over her black fishnet tights.

"That means nobody cares that you have the ski mask. Tonight the crime-watch will decide what to do. It's out of your hands. And I'm doing my act in the audition."

"That's ridiculous. I'm going to tell them you're lying, that Maxine really did it. I'll fix it so that you won't get to do the audition. I'll get you into the most trouble you've ever been in. People will call you the Amazing Valvano, all right. Amazing because you'll be in detention for life."

"You do that and I'll tell Sister Margaret you didn't go right to your tap class last Thursday — you bought candy at Bud's. You'll end up in detention with me."

"How did you find out—"

"I have my ways. However, I'm willing to make a deal. You give me Lester and I forget you went to the candy store."

"But I don't have Lester. Honestly."

It was hard to believe, but Mary Louise actually seemed afraid of me.

"Please don't tell Sister Margaret," she pleaded. "Please."

"You have until the crime-watch meeting tonight." I swaggered to the door. "Good luck at the audition today. Break a leg. And I mean really break it."

"You — you —"

I ran out, leaving Mary Louise sputtering.

"Yahoo!" I yelled when I got outside. Maybe I was going to be punished but Mary Louise was going to get hers, too.

I hurried down the street to Maxine's. When I got to the alley that ran down the side of her house, I saw the cellar door open and Kevin come out of the door holding a cat carrier.

What was Kevin doing here? He was supposed to be at his mom's beauty shop. And another thing: what was he doing with a cat carrier? Kevin didn't have a cat.

I had to get ready for the audition but something told me to follow Kevin. I could be making a mistake, but I had to find out if Lester was in the cat carrier.

I followed Kevin down Russell toward Columbia Road, worrying the whole time. I ducked behind parked cars and crouched in doorways. I even got down on my hands and knees to hide behind a bush. A few times Kevin turned around, but he didn't see me.

When he waited at the bus stop, I hid behind a telephone truck. I knew I couldn't get on the bus without him seeing me so I asked the two telephone workers, "Do you have a real phone on your truck? One that you can call people with?"

"Yes," said one of the workers. "But it's only for emergencies."

"This is an emergency. Someone stole my friend's pet rat and I need him for my magic act. The kidnapper's going to get away on a bus if I don't get help."

"That's a good story," said the other worker, laughing.

"Please," I pleaded. "It's the truth."

"I don't know. That's an unusual emergency," said the first worker.

"Aw, let her call," said the one who laughed.

"Okay." He opened the back panel. My fingers were shaking so much I had to dial Maxine's number three times before I got it right.

I told Maxine to call Joey and get down here right away. They came in less than four minutes. As we walked across the street, the worker who laughed joined us.

I have to hand it to Kevin: he stayed cool. He looked me straight in the eye and said, "What do you want?"

I could only stutter. My throat felt stuck together.

"Give us Lester," yelled Maxine.

"Right now," demanded Joey.

"I don't have him. You must be mistaken."

The worker looked at me. I'd never heard Kevin talk so politely. I said as firmly as I could, "Open that cat carrier."

Kevin opened the cat carrier and in it was . . . Lester? There was a rat in the box, but he had a dark head and a dark blob on his back. The rat stared blankly at us and blinked.

Kevin spoke to the worker in his polite voice. "Her rat was a white laboratory rat, but as you can see this is a hooded rat. I'm sure you can understand: she's upset because she lost her rat. However, this rat is mine." He smiled a thin, cheerless smile.

"Well, what do you say, little girl?" asked the worker. "Is this your rat or not?"

"Excuse me, sir," said Kevin. "Here's my bus. I have an appointment at five-fifteen."

Kevin tried to get past me. My knees felt weak and I thought I was going to cry. Had I come all this way for nothing? Then the rat flicked his tail — a long, hairless, pink tail with a kink in the middle.

Maxine, Joey, and I yelled at the same time, "It's Lester!"

"You can't prove it," snarled Kevin.

Maxine pulled out a reward flier and pointed to the kink in Lester's tail. Lester twitched his nose at us.

"That's him all right," said the worker.

"Hand him over," yelled Joey.

"And give us the props, too," I shouted.

Kevin reverted to his old self and tossed the cat carrier to me, yelling, "Take your stupid rat back."

In the scramble to catch Lester, Kevin escaped.

"Forget him," I shouted. "We're late for the audition."

· 22 ·

The Amazing Valvano

"Jeez, you're brave, Maria," said Ernie as we drove to the audition. "Kevin is one tough kid."

"Thanks, but we should have listened to Maxine, our ace detective. She was right all along about him."

"You're okay, too, Maxine." Ernie turned around and smiled at her. "Anybody know where Kevin was going?"

"He said he had an appointment just after five," said Joey, cuddling Lester in the front seat next to Ernie.

Maxine and I were in the back. I looked through the cat carrier while Maxine wrote our findings in her notebook.

"All our props are here," I said. "There's even a can of sour cherry soda and a piece of jerky." Under my magician's hat I found a business card.

On the front was printed:

BIRTHDAY MAGIC, INC.
CALL US FIRST FOR
CLOWNS, DANCERS, SINGERS & MAGICIANS
HAVE A PARTY THAT'S A *PARTY*
DAY OR NIGHT DIAL: BE-MAGIC

On the back was written: *Wednesday 5:15 — 1408 Telegraph Avenue.*

"Hey! Look at this." I handed the card to Maxine.

"Kevin's handwriting!" she said.

"I've seen their flier," said Joey. "They're hiring. I bet Kevin was trying to get a job with them."

"Or got a job," fumed Maxine. "I wonder if Kevin's been performing our magic act. He was wearing his good pants."

"Jeez, he's got some nerve." Ernie shook his head.

"Been to any parties lately?" Joey asked Lester.

Lester twitched his nose.

"How did he color Lester's hair?" asked Joey.

"There's hair dye that can be combed in," said Maxine.

"That's what your mom used on me," said Ernie.

"That explains why Kevin's hands were so dark the day of the kidnapping," I said. "They were stained from the hair dye. My guess is that Kevin dyed Lester's hair in your parents' shop, Maxine. Remember the mysterious smell in the back room the day of the kidnapping — you thought Kevin broke a bottle?"

"I *totally* agree," said Maxine, writing furiously.

"That's why Ernie's hair had a familiar smell the day my mom knocked over the hydrant," I continued. "And speaking of Mom, she's taking her driver's test right now. I hope she passes."

"Me, too," said Ernie, swerving around a corner.

"I hope the dye won't make Lester sick," said Joey as Lester nuzzled his shoulder.

"Hey, I'm still okay." Ernie reached over and patted Lester.

"You're safe as long as you don't eat it," said Maxine. "Because then you die. Kevin probably tied Lester up till the dye dried. I hope my parents murder him."

"He deserves to be tortured first," said Joey. "You know he borrowed my book on rats. I bet that's where he got the idea of making Lester a hooded rat."

"For starters my parents should ground Kevin for the rest of the year. Then —"

"I'll be grounded for the rest of the year, too, when Mom's crime-watch group gets through with me."

"I'm going to make sure Kevin goes to that meeting, too." Maxine put her hand on my shoulder. "Don't worry. While you're grounded, I'll call you on the phone and come over when your mom is out."

"I'll record songs for you on my tape recorder and send Lester over," said Joey.

Lester twitched his nose as if he liked that. I twitched my nose, too, because I definitely liked that.

"I'll never be bossy again," I promised.

Everyone laughed.

"Hey, don't get carried away," said Ernie.

Joey put Lester into his costume before we went to the audition. He was so happy to have Lester back he even kissed him.

The auditorium was filled with kids from every grade at Saint Anne's and a few parents. Mary Louise and Lily were dancing. They looked great in their costumes, but I was happy to see Mary Louise's mouth hanging open.

"So the superior mind has finally arrived," said Sister Margaret. "It's about time. You're on next."

We set up our props: chair, saw, magic rings, table with tablecloth, and trick box. Lester stayed in the wings with Ernie.

When I got the first mental telepathy question wrong, Mary Louise laughed hilariously and Sister Margaret looked anxious. I calmed everyone by getting the rest of the questions right.

Maxine carried the envelopes, questions, and Joey's clipboard offstage. When she came back, she was wearing my hat with Lester in it. The three of us bowed together, removed our hats, and left them on the chair.

While Joey introduced our last trick, I put my hat on. When he said, "Tonight the Amazing Valvano will saw a rabbit in half," I stepped forward, twirled, bowed, and pulled Lester out of my hat.

Amidst cheers, voices piped: "Isn't he cute." "He's so small." "Why, he's just a bunny." "Oh, no, she's really going to do it." "I can't watch."

Joey wheeled the table with the trick box to the front of the stage and Maxine pushed the chair with the hats behind it.

While I showed Lester to the audience once more, Joey opened the secret panel. Then when I placed Lester in the box, Joey took him right out through the secret panel and put him in my hat, which Maxine was holding. The hat was hidden by the tablecloth as she stood behind the box. Then she put my hat back on the chair with hers and Joey's.

We made a big production of locking snaps and buckling locks. We got a noisy reaction from the audience when we pulled fake rabbit ears from the secret compartment at one end of the box and fake rabbit feet from the compartment at the other end. The audience thought we were really pulling the bunny's ears and feet out.

We spun the table around twice before I inserted the saw. There was deadly silence. I saw Sister Margaret wring her hands. Sister Agnes bowed her head. Ernie gave me a thumbs-up sign from the wings.

I sawed through the sponge. The noise was so sickening some kids covered their eyes. Others covered their mouths. Several parents groaned. I continued until the saw hit the bottom of the box with a sharp thud.

I handed Maxine the saw. We pushed the fake feet and ears back inside the secret compartments. Joey and I put on our hats while Maxine spun the box six times.

Kids were yelling, "Open it. Open it."

Sister Margaret stood up, her hand on her throat.

Sister Agnes covered her face.

I took off the top of the box and Joey tilted it so that everyone could see it was empty. There were gasps and shouts of "Amazing," "Incredible," "How'd she do that?" "Where's the bunny?"

I could see Mom in the audience smiling. She pointed to herself and mouthed, "I passed." Then she pointed to me and mouthed, "You're great." Mrs. Bossi sat next to her, smiling, too.

Once again, I twirled. Then after the deepest possible bow, I pulled Lester out of my hat. The audience cheered, stamped their feet, clapped, and whistled. Even though it was only the audition, we got two curtain calls.

"We did it. We did it," said Maxine as the three of us hugged each other.

Backstage I gave Lester to Joey. "I owe you an apology. I thought you kidnapped Lester. I'm sorry. I was wrong. He's all yours now. I know you love him."

Joey and Lester left with Ernie before Sister Margaret could check the rabbit, but not before Ernie gave me a double thumbs-up sign.

"Your act is thrilling," said Sister Margaret. "You're definitely in the show. And if I'm any judge of talent, you're sure to make the finals."

I couldn't have been any happier. But I knew all along we'd be a hit. After all, I was the Amazing Valvano.